The Perfect Kill Club.

By Martin McGregor.

This book is dedicated to my mother

Brenda McGregor.

You were my teacher, you are my never-ending support, and always will be my inspiration.

I wish that I had just a fraction of the strength and courage that you have, and I beg you to never stop fighting this cruel disease

I can never repay all that you have done for me,

And I love you more than words can say.

Mum, you are my world.

Love from your son.

Martin

The Perfect Kill Club. A story by Martin McGregor

This book was first published in the UK in 2022 by Marlebond Publishing.

ISBN: 9798848845129

Original cover design by Martin McGregor.

Marlebond
Publishing

Also available from this author:

Ellie Caitlin the complete collection

Keep away from the windows

Keep away from the windows 2: The dark ones

Keep away from the windows 3: The world in my eyes

Damaged Goods

24

24: The return

Exit 12

24: The end times

Atlanta Rain

Absolution

Atlanta Rain: Into the Inferno

Atlanta Rain: The Nine Realms

Slide

The Lost Girls

The Hunger Inside

Distorted Visions

Distorted Visions: The Killing Jar

Distorted Visions: Insomnia

Distorted Visions: The Heart of Twilight

The Order

Portal

Introduction

During a rather dull winter's day at work, I suddenly had a rather crazy idea for a story that popped into my head from out of nowhere, and then it began to fester. Over lunch, the idea seemed to take shape even further, so I decided to run it past my friend who, on hearing the premise seemed rather keen and quite excited by the idea. The basic premise for The Perfect Kill Club was born on that day, and since it involved elements of time travel, it has given me a major headache ever since.

The story's first draft took me a little less than a week to complete. As for the work required and the changes needed on the second draft, let's just say that it took me quite a while longer. Despite my best intentions life just seemed to get in the way of my creativity once again. The story went in a few different directions, and even when it was complete, it still felt like something was missing.

Then my mother was diagnosed with Cancer for a second time, and it put things into perspective about how fragile life is, and what we must endure as human beings. Since her first dose of chemotherapy, she has struggled, and I wanted to finish this book in tribute to her bravery and courage and to give her something to look forward to. Here it is Mum, this book is just for you.

This story is about the perils of time travel, and how it would affect the future if you made changes to the past, or maybe this is a story about how those changes would not affect the future at all. I had to try and work out a way to not cause ripples in the future, but I had to use a fair amount of artistic license in the way that the characters jumped backwards and forward through time.

Are you confused yet? If you aren't then you soon will be. If I said any more, then I would give the game away, so I will let you take a read of my latest creation from my warped imagination and see for yourself. I hope that you enjoy it.

Martin

I would like to say an enormous heartfelt thank you to the following people:

Heather and Sean Swinson for all your never-ending help and support. You are appreciated! My mother Brenda, has always been my biggest fan. My sons, Nick, Chris, Jordan and Owen. My grandchildren, Freddie, Bobby, Marley, Dahlia and Ace, for all the joy you give me. To Tracey Elena, Morgana Moon and Shean Christopher for your support and encouragement and for sharing in my madness.

Thank you, my regular readers, including Jennifer Bastholm, Denise Patient, Jazz Sawyer, Jazz Dixon, Judith Monk, Tracey Ware, Andy Turner, Ali and Mark Gibbs, Maurice Sweeney, Jeanne Campbell, Andy Oliver, Steve Bodsworth, Maggi and Andrew and to all my readers who enjoy sharing in the madness I create. My heartfelt thanks go out to you all.

Now it is time to go back, time to see the future past.

Enjoy!

Martin McGregor. August 2022.

7th January 1943.

The loss of the greatest mind of all time.

The evening was warmer than usual for the time of year, and on the 33rd floor of the Hotel New Yorker, the apartment's sole elderly resident was falling asleep in his favourite chair. He had stayed at this hotel for quite some time, as it felt like a home to him. He would often wake in the early hours of the morning in this very same spot, before slowly making his way to bed. He had moved from cheap hotel to cheap hotel over the last few years, but from the moment he first opened the apartment door, he knew that this would be the last room he would ever stay in.

He loved this place because, during his stay here, he was able to use the lift to travel down to the ground floor and then take a short walk down to the corner of 40th street and Sixth Avenue, where he would take some time to feed the pigeons. He loved the birds as unlike the many humans he had trusted over the course of his lifetime, the birds were pure of heart, and they never meant him any harm. Sometimes when he talked to the birds, he wished that they could reply, so he could see how the birds thought.

He never forgot the friendship he had forged with a pure, white-coloured pigeon that he had grown attached to many years back. The birds were innocent and would never betray him in the ways that his former colleagues had. Feeding the birds had given him a sense of purpose and helped him to overcome his loneliness after his wife had sadly passed away.

The elderly man was comfortably heading into a deep sleep when he was awoken suddenly, by a series of three gentle knocks on the wooden door of his hotel room. It was dark outside of the window, reflecting the lateness of the hour and it was unusual for anyone to come to his room at this time of night. Nikola Tesla struggled as he tried to get up from his chair, but finally, he managed to stand up.

The pain in his leg was becoming unbearable, but at his age, the feeling of pain in one or more of his limbs was nothing new to him. He suddenly experienced the strangest feeling of Deja vu, and he realised that he had seen this moment in time before. Despite the growing sense of dread, that was sending butterflies rampaging through his chest, he was determined to greet his unexpected visitor, even if it were the grim reaper coming to take him at this time of the night.

The sound of the knocking on the door came again, only this time the sound was a little louder and more hurried, as the visitor became more demanding of a response from the room's sole occupant. This was some urgent business that needed his attention.

"Alright, alright, I'm coming! Please be patient, I am eighty-six years old and although my body is willing, my limbs are no longer capable of moving forward at any great speed!" The old man shouted out loud and smiled to himself at what he had said, hoping that the visitor would refrain from knocking again as he shuffled forwards toward the door.

His body ached all over with each step the pain intensified, and Tesla knew that the time of his demise was close at hand. He did not fear death, he had already seen the future and he knew the pain and despair that it held for humanity. War, pestilence and disease would become rife. Despite all the world-changing advances in the realms of science, they would mean nothing.

If left unchecked, mankind would succumb to increasing greed which would eventually consume all the planet's resources and destroy all its native species in the animal kingdom. A war to end all wars was soon to become inevitable. A peaceful death was preferable to living through the mess that mankind was now hurtling towards at an increasingly unrelenting speed.

The old man turned the lock with his aged fingers and opened the door up just wide enough for him to peer around the edge, enabling him to see who had come here to visit him at this late hour. Outside in the hallway, there was a young man dressed in a smart black suit. He was searching all around. His eyes darted left and right, looking nervously at the doors to the other rooms and the elevator doors on this floor as if expecting one of them to open any second.

The old man sighed as he realised that he had seen his visitor's face before, and now he began to have mixed feelings as he came to accept that his life was nearly over. His time here on Earth was truly almost done. The butterflies in his chest swarmed and would not still. The elderly man knew that he had just hours left to live at most.

"Can I help you?" The old man asked.

The suited man in the hallway was sweating slightly, and he continued to look all around him nervously. He was worried that someone might have followed him here, and they might drag him away at any second.

"Mr Tesla, you do not know me, but I am here to beg for your help. Can I come inside for a few moments, please? It is extremely urgent. I need to speak with you about a matter of grave importance. This is to do with one of your inventions." His voice sounded desperate, he seemed scared.

Tesla examined his face. There were signs of real desperation in the man's eyes. The old man slowly absorbed the stranger's words, and then Tesla began to chuckle to himself.

"My dear boy, I have created many wonderful things throughout my lifetime, and yet here I am, living alone in this single room. I am penniless and with nothing to show for my creations. Now I have only my beloved pigeons for company.

Others have taken the credit or have suppressed the ideas, that I created to aid humanity to progress and thrive, but instead have been used to exploit mankind purely for financial gain, which has defeated my spirit. Now I am far too old to care about the hand that life has dealt me, so I will bid you a good evening, sir, and I wish you every luck with your quest. Now I must return to my bed, for a much-needed sleep."

The old man was just about to shut the hotel room's door when the stranger jammed his foot inside of the frame to prevent it from being closed. He held on to the door tightly as he spoke again, with more urgency in his voice. There was no point in Tesla trying to force the door closed, as he was old and weak, and this man's grip was far too strong. The stranger knew that this was his only chance to try and find a way to prevent what was about to happen, so he came straight to the point in the hope that Tesla might understand the sheer gravity of the situation.

“They are going ahead with the invisibility experiment that you warned them about! I know you told them it was too dangerous to attempt, but a military research team has spent the last few months creating and fitting numerous giant coils to a large navy ship. Those coils were based on your designs. With the coils engaged, they will try to render a warship invisible and then attempt to take it back in time. I know that you walked away from the research after warning the government against going ahead with this experiment, but they are determined to push forward with it anyway, no matter what the risk is.”

The old man shook his head in utter disbelief at what he was hearing. He opened the door so that the gap was wide enough to allow his guest to see him standing in the dim light of the hotel room. The once welcoming smile on Tesla’s face had now disappeared. It was hard to believe that this frail old man with sunken cheekbones had been such a brilliant inventor or the harsh hand that life had dealt him.

Tesla sighed in sheer desperation.

“If that is the case, then I guess you had better come inside for a moment so that we may discuss this matter further.” Tesla held the door wide open allowing the man to step inside, and he breathed a sigh of relief. As he entered the hotel room Tesla locked the door behind them both.

“Thank you.” Tesla could understand why his visitor was so anxious now.

“I know that this is not the most luxurious hotel room, and I have little to offer my guests in terms of refreshments, but please, do take a seat.” The old man offered, and the suited man sat down on a cushioned wooden chair, as he looked around him, surveying everything within the hotel room.

Aside from a bed, some cheap ornaments and a few pieces of furniture, the small room was almost bare inside. Tesla moved slowly across the floor heading towards his favourite seat.

“Now then, I want you to tell me a little more about what you say they are going to attempt to do with this ship.” The old man’s bones creaked as he eased himself down so that he was sitting directly opposite his guest who in turn edged forward in his seat before nervously clearing his throat.

“The men in charge of this project want to use your invention to try and change the course of warfare. They took the initial designs that you submitted and after consulting with Einstein and many other scientists, they have adapted your designs to try and increase the power output. They have enlarged the coils you created and grouped them to become substantial enough, that they now think it will give them the power to enable them to make an entire warship invisible and then transport it back through time."

The old man shook his head in disbelief at what he was hearing. The invention he had submitted was not designed to be used in this way.

"They are dangerous fools! I warned them repeatedly that time travel should never be attempted. To go back and change anything in the past could destroy the future by tearing apart the very fabric of our existence! They do not know what they are messing with. If they do harness enough power to achieve Quantum teleportation of something as large as a warship, it will only serve to merge everything and everyone on that boat into one object at a cellular level.

Their atoms will blend into one form, and God only knows what fate will befall the crew of that vessel. I can assure you that it will not be pleasant. You must try and stop them from ever attempting this ludicrous experiment. If they go ahead, then they will bring only misery and death to everyone on board that ship."

"They are determined to go ahead with this crazy idea regardless of what anyone says. For some reason, they are convinced that they can travel back through time and use this ship to alter the course of history, but surely time travel cannot become a reality, by the very laws of the universe, it must be impossible?"

"No. I can assure you that is perfectly achievable. I know as I have seen the future with my own eyes." Tesla looked saddened by his revelation.

The old man stood up from his chair and slowly made his way over to the dressing table that he was using as a makeshift desk. Napkins lay neatly folded in a stack on top of it. The pile was eighteen in number, and it had to be eighteen exactly. To the left of the desk, there were nine piles of notes stacked in groups of six which were placed tidily in a specific order. The numbers three, six, nine and eighteen were extremely important to him.

Tesla leaned over and took two files from the top of one pile and pulled another one out from close to the bottom of a different stack. He breathed a sigh of relief when the rest of the stack didn't topple over, and he wouldn't have to pick them up again. Then he opened a drawer and added empty files to both stacks so that each was six high again. The number of files had to remain consistent.

The elderly man then turned around and held out the three files in his hand. He looked saddened as he handed them over to his suited visitor. Almost as if he were giving away a part of his soul. His hand was shaking badly in the air as he passed them across to their new owner.

"The green files on the top contain the full instructions on how to create two of my inventions. You can sell these detailed instructions to the highest bidder, and the money you make from the sales should be more than enough for you to fund the creation of the machine inside of the orange file. The solution that you seek to any problem that may occur if this goes ahead, is inside of there.

You can take these files with my blessing, on the understanding that you keep this creation out of the hands of the undeserving, and that you promise me that this machine is only to be used for the good of mankind. The knowledge that is contained in there, will allow you to go back and correct any further mistakes that they make in the future with their infernal meddling."

The suited man gratefully accepted the files and opened them one at a time slowly flipping through the handwritten pages and drawings contained in each folder. He spent a few moments examining the contents. Inside the large, orange-coloured file, there were pages and pages of complex mathematical equations followed by many more pages with detailed instructions on how to build a complex self-contained machine, along with the knowledge of how to create a minimalist plasma field.

The design was for a machine that would protect a traveller who could port backwards and forward through time from within the sealed containment unit.

"I don't understand. It says here that these are plans for a time machine. So, let me get this straight. Are you telling me that when this is built, someone can use this machine to travel back through time and what they are trying to achieve is possible?" Tesla smiled and nodded his head to confirm his guest's assumption was correct.

"It is more than possible, for a single person I can assure you that this design will work and make it a reality for them to traverse back, but it would not work for anything like a large inanimate object such as a warship. Even so, you must always consider that there are great risks associated with interfering in any affairs of the past. I cannot stress this point strongly enough."

"Why don't you give these files over to someone in your family or a close friend? Surely there must be someone more suited to take care of these important plans, other than surrendering things as important as these over to a stranger?"

The old man sat back in his chair and stared up at the ceiling.

"I have a good feeling about you. You came here to stop them, and that is how I know that I can trust you. I no longer have the time to reach out to anyone else. Because of your visit, I know that tomorrow is my last day on this Earth, and I am ready to take my much-earned rest."

"But, how can you say that with such certainty?" The suited man was shaking his head in confusion at what Tesla was trying to tell him. It was as if this brilliant inventor had foreknowledge that his death was imminent.

"I told you how. I know, because I have already travelled through time. I discovered that the past present and future are all intertwined. When I die, the government are going to come into this hotel room and take away most of my work. They will keep my idea for free energy locked away. All the other advancements I had invented for the good of all mankind, will be suppressed by the rich and powerful too.

I may die penniless, but I am content with all that I have achieved in my life. Now I am afraid that I must ask you to leave me in peace to ready myself for my final journey. I would like to take some time alone to reflect on the happier moments of my life."

The suited man stood up from the chair and held out his hand in a show of respect for this brilliant scientist and decent human being. Tesla put out his frail hand and met his guest's open palm. The two men shook hands, and Tesla knew from the firmness of his grip, that this man could be trusted, and that he too had a good heart.

"Thank you for giving me the chance to do this. I will do all that I can to stop them." The suited man said as he held the file out in front of him.

"I know that you will." He replied, knowing full well that nothing could change the future he had already seen, but at least his plans would now be safe for a while, hidden away from prying eyes.

“It’s been a pleasure to meet you, Mr Tesla. I will see myself out.” The suited man walked to the door of the apartment and unlocked it. He checked the hallway again, to make sure that it was clear, closing the door softly behind him as he left.

The following morning Nikola Tesla’s nephew Sasa Kosanovic, received a phone call, informing him that his uncle Nikola had sadly passed away in his room in the early hours of the morning. He made his way to the New Yorker hotel as quickly as he could. He took the elevator up to the 33rd floor where a concierge met him and gave him access to the room, so that he may show his respects, and collect any items left behind.

As Sasa entered the room, it looked immaculately clean. There was no sign of his late uncle left to be seen. Most of Tesla’s notes and files were missing from the hotel room as well.

Flash forward

On the 28th of October 1943 in Philadelphia, the generators started and fed power to the coils on the USS Eldridge. An eerie green and blue glow surrounded the hull of the ship before it vanished into thin air. The ship briefly reappeared in the Norfolk naval shipyard in Virginia, before it vanished again and then it reappeared in Philadelphia.

When the scientists and the military officers boarded the vessel, they were greeted by scenes of absolute horror. Just as Tesla had predicted, the atoms of the ship and its crew had become intertwined. Various crewmen were found embedded within the metallic elements of the craft. Eyes stared out blindly from the walls, fingers probed from the ceiling, while various other body parts were randomly interspersed throughout the ship. Others had parts of the vessel embedded inside of their bodies.

Part of a port hole had been merged with a sailor's head, with the bolts driven deep into his brain. Another was found with pieces of the ship's outer cladding protruding from his flesh, and the cladding had become fused to his bones. A sailor lay screaming from his injuries as he lay in a pool of oil that was leaking out from his deep wounds, a propeller blade slicing through his head. The crewmen who were unlucky enough to still be alive had all been rendered insane.

The experiment was abandoned there and then. The results were kept locked away in secrecy so that engineers could continue to work on the technology as advances in the world of science evolved.

Into The Future Past.

The settings on the machine were all securely fixed and locked into place. The safety switches were activated before Alexander stepped up to the front of the cylindrical machine, and then he turned around to face the operator, who was standing over at the controls.

“Are you ready to go back and play now Alexander?” Olivia asked, while the rest of the club eagerly awaited his departure.

“I am more than ready for this!” He replied enthusiastically.

“Then you must repeat the rules of the game to me before I execute the jump command,” Olivia told him. It was a chore for all the members to have to repeat the rules to her every time they were chosen to jump, but they were a necessary evil that everyone needed to remember. They all needed to adhere to them to the letter. The future of all life on Earth might depend on it.

Alexander took a deep breath, sighing deeply before he began his recital of the rules. Olivia could tell from his tone, that he was bored with this repetitive inconvenience. He was eager to get on with the game.

“There is to be no intentional interaction with anyone other than the intended victim. Scores from the game will only count if an original method of execution occurs, no repetition of a previous method of termination will be accepted and if this occurs, the participant would not be given a score and would have to pay a financial forfeit if a correction must be made. All members must be aware of the butterfly effect and the repercussions of an unclean attempt, or of a failed kill.

I hereby promise to leave and jump forward immediately once the task is completed, without taking any souvenirs of the visit. God save the Queen." The last part was an ad-lib that Alexander added purely for comedic effect, and it made the members laugh. The rules themselves were pretty much self-explanatory, and the game was ready to begin.

"Congratulations. You may now step inside of the vessel." Olivia told him. She was smiling wide. History was about to be re-written once again.

Alexander moved forward so that he was facing the rear of the vessel and after drawing his breath, he turned around inside of the machine. He had put on a fair bit of weight recently, and the space was becoming tighter inside. The door closure mechanism fired noisily as it began to lower until it covered him fully, and then the locks were sealed in place. Alexander placed his hands around the hold on the wall, and he closed his eyes as he waited for the plasma flood to occur.

Olivia activated the power switch on the panel and the countdown timer started at the number five and then descended to the count of one which was when the machine would become active.

"You have the maximum allowed time of fifteen minutes to complete the game, and you must activate the return in the event of an emergency. Happy hunting, and may your score be a record beater. I wish you every success in your quest to attain the perfect kill. I know that you can do this!" She told him encouragingly.

To Olivia, each trip through time that she sent the members on, was just as exciting as the last. As the speaker on the counter sounded out the number one, an electrical charge burst through the cylinder and Alexander arched his back. He looked upward, ready to begin his quest, and he felt exhilarated as his journey into the past began.

Within seconds, the room was filled with a brilliant flash of electric blue light as the plasma became charged and when the light had faded, he was gone. He had a little less than a quarter of an hour to complete the task, and then get out, but this time around, he was determined to beat the other nineteen members of the club. He was desperate to win the grand prize awarded to the first member of the club who achieved the perfect score. The prize on offer amounted to a colossal five billion pounds which were held in an offshore account.

Awake

Outside of the house, Sharon walked the length of the front garden as the sun was starting to rise high above the rooftops in the early morning sky. It was almost five a.m. Sharon inhaled deeply, breathing in the cool morning air that filled her lungs, as she began the short walk back toward her home. She had spent the previous evening enjoying a movie session at her friend Debbie's house.

The night before, the pair of long-time friends had wound down with a relaxing evening, filled with laughter as they watched trashy rom-com movies while eating pizza and spiced potato wedges together. They would visit each other's homes frequently, alternating between houses. Spending time together helped both relax and unwind after a tough week. If it had been a super tough week for either of them, they would share a few glasses of wine as well.

Sharon had an unwritten rule that she had always abided by. She would always leave her car at home if she was going to partake in drinking any alcohol at all, and there were no exceptions to this rule. Even though she had only consumed two glasses of sparkling wine throughout the entire evening, she would not have been tempted to step into her car. It was the one rule that she stuck to rigidly, and she would always refuse to drive after consuming any food or drink that had alcohol in it at all, even a portion of sherry trifle.

Despite her best intentions to leave the house around midnight and then return home, Sharon had fallen asleep on Debbie's sofa during the second movie they had chosen to stream. As she looked exhausted but comfortable where she was, Debbie decided not to wake her. Instead, she had covered her up with her spare duvet and then she had made her way up to bed.

Birdsong had woken Sharon up on the sofa around four in the morning. She was a little disorientated at first until she realised that she was still on the sofa in Debbie's living room. She deliberated, but then decided against calling a taxi, as it would be a nightmare trying to get one at this time of the morning. The walk to her home was a relatively short one anyway, and it was the middle of June, and the early morning weather outside was comfortably warm, even at this early hour.

After folding up the duvet neatly and placing it on the sofa, Sharon searched around the living room until she found a pen and a piece of paper, to write out a little thank you note. She left this on the sofa on top of the duvet for when Debbie woke up. Sharon let herself out of the house and gently closed the front door behind her as quietly as possible so as not to disturb anyone. Debbie's elderly neighbours in the house to her right were funny at the best of times, so waking them up this early would be a very bad idea.

The fastest way for Sharon to make her way back home was for her to head down the hill, and then turn left on London Road. From there she could walk through the town centre, passing through the middle of Andover high street and then take a shortcut through by the college. This route was the quickest way back to her house, but it would take her around the stinky duck pond by the old magistrate's court. In the summer heat, the pond water became a little on the pungent side.

As she made her way down the hill, the occasional car drove past her, but there were very few other people awake at this time in the morning. As Sharon walked through the town centre, she found that it was eerily quiet, aside from the melodic sounds of birdsong from the rooftops. There was a gentle rustle of a discarded plastic bag as it was propelled along the ground by a soft summer breeze.

From a deep recess in her mind, she began thinking about the floating plastic islands in the Oceans. The discarded bag would probably make its way into the river and then possibly to the sea. She picked it up and placed it in the bin instead. Looking around, there was a lot of discarded rubbish on the floor and half-eaten food from drunken revellers that was now being devoured by hungry pigeons. Humans could be worse than animals sometimes.

Sharon could now see the focal point in the distance, as she walked up toward the familiar sight of St Mary's church, located at the top of the town. She walked past the small number of retail shops that were all that remained of a once thriving shopping centre. These few stores would be closed for the next few hours until the Sunday trading hours began, but there were very few visitors to the shops early on Sunday mornings.

There were several empty retail units in the town, but the amount of 'To Let' signs hanging over the shops seemed to be growing in number by the week, and it was sad to see the gradual demise of the precinct, due to high rents and the growing rise in popularity of online shopping. The town's population had continued to expand, but the facilities had never managed to keep pace.

As she reached the top of the town, Sharon turned left at the Golden Dragon Chinese restaurant. She stared into the window at the fancy décor, and reading the menu made her feel hungry. After a moment of hesitation, she walked down the hill past Rigby's barbers and continued towards the town sports centre. As she reached the turning on the right to the shortcut through by the pond, she almost jumped out of her skin. There was a barrage of sounds that came at her from a large flock of

Canadian geese that were hidden from view, just around the corner. It felt like they had been waiting to ambush her.

The birds all began to squawk noisily at Sharon, and she recoiled in horror at the unexpected sight of the flock. The size of these birds was frightening and the sheer number of them gathered in such a small area, was incredible. Sharon stepped back to the path and decided to change her course. She would have to walk around the birds instead of cutting through them, bypassing the pond by the Lights Theatre. She walked the long way around to the pathway instead which ended up taking her out by the underpass beneath the dual carriageway.

Sharon was now about to embark on the final part of the journey that would take her home. Her house was about a five-minute walk from the main road. All she had to do, was to walk through the darkened underpass and she would emerge on the opposite side of the dual carriageway and close to the site of the old Andover workhouse. Her home was just along to the right of that building, which had now been converted into flats, burying elements of the dark history of the building's past.

Far behind her, the geese were still harping away noisily at each other, and now that there was a safe distance between her and the birds, Sharon could afford to laugh to herself at just how frightened she had been when she had first encountered the animals. She turned left towards the underpass and continued walking into the shadowed area under the bridge. The lights in the ceiling underneath the bridge appeared to have been vandalised yet again. No doubt the damage had been done by some mindless idiots who thought that they were being clever by destroying council property for fun.

Sharon was still smiling to herself about the birds and shaking her head at her stupidity. The birds were probably more scared of her than she of them, and she should have continued walking through them, and they would have dispersed. Now she started giggling while embarking on the final stretch toward her home. She was almost at Junction Road and her house was just around the next corner.

Suddenly, Sharon felt pain in her head as her hair was yanked forcefully back. In her confused state, and with pain searing through her scalp, she found herself struggling to stay upright. Just a few seconds ago, she had been looking back and there had been no one at all even close to her. She spun around on her heels wondering just what the hell was happening.

A large blonde man stood menacingly in front of her. Even though she had spun around, he had managed to keep hold of her hair as he gripped it tightly with his left hand. Sharon noticed that he was holding something shiny in his other hand that was glinting in the sun. The man swung his right hand up so that it was above his head, and then he plunged it down toward her skull.

Instinctively, Sharon raised her hand in front of her face to try and protect herself. The sharp knife that the man was brandishing, sliced through her middle finger, almost severing it completely. The force of the momentum from the swing, carried the blade down further until it was wedged deep into her palm.

It took a few seconds for her brain to register what had just happened to her, but then Sharon screamed out loud as the agonizing pain of the injury finally kicked in. The blade that was still embedded in her hand was painful enough, but the severed finger was stinging so badly that it was difficult to know which was the most serious wound. She blinked back her tears, and in desperation, she struck out with her foot and successfully managed to catch the man square in his shin. Then she repeated the kick as hard as she could.

The man yelped out loud as he felt the blows to his leg and then he backed off slightly. Suddenly Sharon realised that he had let go of her hair. She edged a few steps back while turning away from him, and now she was going to attempt to try and run away from her attacker. She knew that this man wanted to kill her, and he was doing everything in his power to make her suffer.

The stocky male wasn't quite finished with Sharon yet. As she began to run, he realised that time was of the essence, and he could not afford to let her escape. At the last second, he lunged forward and caught her around the midriff. The weight of the man against the small of her back sent her off balance and he bundled Sharon down onto the pavement. She felt the rough surface of the pavement as it grazed her all along on side of her face, and the cuts began to sting almost immediately.

The impact from falling onto the tarmac path had knocked the air from her lungs and the relentless assailant quickly jumped up and sat on top of her stomach, to stop her from moving around so much. He was desperate to retrieve the knife that was still embedded in Sharon's hand, but the target was fighting him back, and this wasn't part of his plan.

“Why won’t you just stay still and die you fucking bitch?” He screamed out loud at her.

Sharon could see that the man was out of shape. His breathing was heavy, and his brow was covered in sweat. He looked afraid. She had never seen this man before, and Sharon had no idea why he was trying to kill her.

“Fuck you! Get off me, you bastard!” Sharon screamed, and then she heard a voice close by that seemed to come out of nowhere.

“Warning! This is a proximity alert. You now have sixty seconds to complete the mission before this scenario is compromised by a third-party witness.” The voice appeared to have come from a device on the man's wrist. The distraction allowed the assailant the few seconds that he needed.

There was a moment of immense pain and Sharon screamed as the knife was finally ripped out of her hand. The man seemed frantic and desperate to end her life as he continued with his relentless and frenzied attack. Sharon tried to fight him back, but with his weight on top of her, it was futile. Her strength was beginning to wane.

The man plunged the knife repeatedly into Sharon's chest. Despite the pain, and the overwhelming urge to sleep, she was still desperately trying to save herself. She wanted to live long enough to see her family and friends once more and the thought of never seeing them again gave her a sudden surge of strength to try and protect herself. Sharon raised her hands time and time again to try and absorb or deflect some of the blows, but by now, she had lost a lot of blood, and life was starting to drain from her eyes as her body became weaker.

The device on the man's wrist issued another important message.

"Final warning. You have just fifteen seconds to complete the mission. A fatal blow to the target is now required." The device warned, and the blonde man knew that he was rapidly running out of time. This game was over, and a life-ending injury to the girl was required.

Lacking in time, he immediately sliced the knife straight across Sharon's throat, cutting her windpipe and as the wound opened, his clothes were splattered with arterial sprays of her blood.

"The fatal blow has been executed. The subject will not survive. You may now safely activate the return." Alexander did not waste any time. He hit the button on his watch, and there was a flash of bright blue light as a plasma field formed around him, and then he was gone. There was no incriminating evidence left behind that anyone else had ever been in the area, and it would be a mystery that would baffle the police.

Sharon lay on the cold tarmac pavement, and she could feel the blood pumping as it escaped from the wounds in her neck and hand. She attempted to cough and tried to clear her throat, but despite her best efforts, there was nothing more than a weak gurgling sound coming out of her mouth. The thick coppery fluid quickly filled her mouth and lungs. Her body convulsed a few times before it began to shut down.

Just at that very moment, a teenage boy riding on his bike was heading toward Sharon. He had a paper bag hung over his shoulder, and he seemed to be in a real hurry. As the boy drew closer, he stopped and stared down in horror at Sharon who looked to be in a complete mess. She was now too weak to even raise her hand. The boy had never seen someone who looked so badly injured before in his life, and the sight of her struggling as she lay dying, was terrifying to him.

Her eyes stared up at him and they were pleading with him to save her, but there was nothing that he could do. She looked afraid of what was about to happen next. Sharon knew that she was dying, and her short life had been relatively uneventful. She had dreams of a successful career in medicine and then starting a family one day, and she was not yet ready to accept the inevitable. Then her breathing stopped, and her left leg twitched nervously as numerous trails of crimson blood slowly ran out from underneath her body.

The boy watched on frozen in terror, but unable to take his eyes away as the blood flowed in straight lines from underneath the woman, heading down the incline of the path until it edged over the kerb and then it dropped into the road where it pooled together.

"Fucking hell." The boy said before throwing the paper bag he'd been carrying aside and then cycling away. He was making his way toward his parent's house as fast as he could pedal. He was going to try and get the woman some help, not knowing that he was already far too late to save her life.

Reverb.

The time correction agency had completed its main mission and it was about to be made obsolete. The agency had just two offices, one of which was in the United States and the other one was situated in London England. Officially, the agency did not exist, and it would not be found listed on any official documents. Its very existence was reliant on funding that came from an unknown source.

Many suspected that it was a secretive billionaire inventor who was providing the funding for the agency and who was responsible for putting an end to time travel, due to the potential danger it posed to mankind. The last known time machine in the entire world had just been destroyed in the United States less than a week ago. The agents in both countries had all been informed that they would be assigned to various other posts where possible.

The secret department had been formerly tasked with fixing any problems that occurred as a result of a third party corrupting the time continuum. Then they were ordered to destroy all-time devices and seize any design plans. Tesla's gifts had indeed been sold for enough money to create a time travel device, but more than one machine was created by the engineer, and these machines had both disappeared, never to be seen again.

The CIA had obtained secret copies of the Tesla plans and they had also developed newer versions of the device in the nineteen seventies. These plans were shared with British intelligence as this was the most successful out of the seven different methods of time travel that they had experimented with. Many of these machines the government had created had since fallen into the wrong hands, but Brandon and the other agents had been determined to destroy them all. At long last, it was mission accomplished.

Brandon Lee was the only agent to have successfully time travelled on more than fifty different occasions, without suffering from any of the usual nasty side effects. The first trip that any agent ever attempted was a short jump back that took them five minutes into the past. The initial journeys back through time were normally a complete success and they were conducted under strictly controlled parameters.

The return trip was what could only be described as 'extremely unpleasant on the senses,' and would occasionally leave the traveller throwing up inside of the plasma chamber from the moment they had completed their return jump. The delayed effects of temporal displacement would affect most people a few hours after they returned, and largely in all the same ways. They suffered from nausea, projectile vomiting, diarrhoea that ranged from mild to explosive and a few days suffering from vertigo. As such most of the potential agents refused to jump for a second time.

For all his many faults, to everyone who knew him, Brandon was a man of high integrity. He would never have gone back in time to alter the course of the future for his personal gain, he would only ever go back to correct mistakes that were related to the timeline fractures. Time travel infringements had become far more common, despite most of the general public being unaware that such technology had even existed.

A few of the earliest unauthorised trips into the past had caused huge ripples resulting in what would soon become known as 'The Mandela effect'. Sometimes these errors were impossible to correct, and Brandon was the senior agent who had been tasked with tracking down and destroying any unauthorised time travel technology. It was a job that he loved, as he knew that it was making a difference.

With the development of quantum computing, it was now possible to calculate when ripples in the past had occurred, no matter how small they were, and for the agents to go back to a point in time before the events and prevent the ripples before they could ever happen. It was just a matter of time before a major catastrophic event occurred, and The Time Correction agents now believed that they had tracked down what was left of the remaining time machines and had destroyed them all.

Brandon lived alone and he had no attachments, which was perfect considering the risks related to his profession. Today was Friday, and he had been given the day off from work as due to the lack of machines left to destroy, the business had been a little slow of late. He was awoken from a pleasant dream by the sound of an incoming video call. His eyes opened wide, and he sat bolt upright in his bed. It was just gone nine in the morning.

Brandon leaned over and pressed the answer call button on the touchscreen. The face of Samantha Proud filled the screen. Her hair looked perfect, with not a single strand looking out of place.

“Good morning, Brandon. I hope that I didn't wake you?” Her smile was a pleasant one.

“Morning. Yes, you did, but it's fine. I wanted to be at the gym soon anyway. I thought that you told us to take the day off. Is there a problem?” He asked, his face filled with confusion about the reason for her call.

“I know that we thought our mission to destroy the time travel devices was complete, but an issue has developed outside of our usual parameters. One that does not impact future timelines, but I believe that you would still be interested in correcting these situations.”

“We’re not talking about an Ellie Caitlin-style scenario again here, are we?” Samantha gave a little chuckle at the question. Ms Caitlin had managed to travel far into the future and then back into the past and in doing so, had almost caused the end of the world.

“No, it's nothing like that.” She assured him.

“I don't know why you find it so funny. She could have destroyed the planet!”

“She could have, but she made it right. That is all that matters. No, this man has handed himself in voluntarily. He says that he has a time machine that was designed by none other than Tesla himself. This could lead us to both of those fabled machines at last. Anyway, I need you to come into the office and just listen to what this guy has to say. He wants to offer us a deal in return for handing over the device. What time do you think that you can get here?”

Brandon looked at the smartwatch on his wrist. It was just gone five minutes past nine. He wasn’t sure that he wanted to take on another mission, as he was looking forward to not having to jump back through time again, but he had a feeling that he may just have to. The chance to locate the two legendary machines was important, so he would have to put off his gym visit until some point later in the day.

“I think that I can be with you by ten.”

“That's fine. Meet me in my office. I can't wait for you to hear all about this one. I think you are going to want to deal with this quite quickly.”

“To be honest, now you say that it’s giving me a bad vibe. Why do I not like the sound of this job?” Samantha just smiled at him.

“If you are reluctant, then I can always involve another agent?” She suggested.

“No. It doesn’t matter. I will see you at ten.” He confirmed and then he ended the video call.

Brandon jumped out of bed and turned his phone's music player on and set it at full volume. He took some clean clothes from the drawers and wardrobe while he listened to the sound of Bring me the Horizon blaring through the phone’s speaker. Then he walked briskly towards the shower. A few minutes of cold water running over his body from the powerful water jets while he sang along to the song ‘Kingslayer’ would be just the tonic to wake him up properly, and the loud volume of this music was just what he needed to kickstart his day.

Scoreboard.

Alexander seemed impatient as the transport tube slowly lifted, and as he stepped out from inside of the chamber and the plasma around him dissipated, he looked visibly angry.

“What the hell just happened back there?” Olivia asked him. She looked sheepish as she asked the question, but Alexander wasn’t in the mood for playing games anymore.

“Oh, come on woman, you already bloody know! I want you to show me what my mistakes have cost me on the leader board.” He demanded. Olivia shook her head.

“I don't think that it's a good idea. I think you should just forget this one. You made the kill in the end and didn’t need another member to recover the mission, so you can put this mission down to a bad experience. You know there will be plenty of other chances to go back and achieve a better score!”

“Don't bloody patronise me, you stupid woman! What if someone achieves the perfect kill and wins the game before my next turn comes around?” He was so angry with her, that spittle flew out from his lips as he bellowed. “I paid an absolute fortune for membership of the club, now I demand that you show me my score before I really do lose my temper!”

Olivia was growing fed up with Alexander's sulky attitude towards her. She was just trying to make it easier on him and soften the blow. This wasn’t the first time he had struggled with the kill, and she was annoyed with his attitude toward her when this wasn’t her fault. He was the one who messed it up, but she was the one being unfairly subjected to his aggressive manner.

“Fine. Suit yourself. Don't say that I didn't warn you.” She snapped back at him.

Olivia held out a headset towards Alexander who rudely snatched it out from between her hands and hurriedly placed it over the top of his head.

“Display kill parameters.” He said into the mouthpiece. The television news report from the day of the murder then appeared on the headset, and then played out on the three-dimensional display that covered his eyes.

He had seen this reporter’s broadcast repeatedly during the last few years. Each time the report was a slightly different one, depending on the inventiveness and method of the kill. The reporter’s voice filled his ears.

‘It was here in this underpass that twenty-one-year-old Sharon Curtis was found by a passer-by early this morning. When she was discovered, she had suffered a severe injury to the hand, almost severing a finger and then her throat had been cut. There are no apparent motives for the brutal attack. Emergency services attended, but the victim was pronounced dead at the scene.

Police are appealing for any witnesses who may have been in the area at the time or who may have seen the victim as she made her way from Shepherds Row, through the town centre or by the sports centre. If you have any information that may be of use or dash-cam footage that may help to shed some light on this incident, then they urge you to please come forward to assist them with their enquiries as soon as possible.'

Alexander's face was now a deep shade of purple. He ripped off the headset and threw it angrily across the room. It struck the wall, and the impact was so hard, that it fell to the floor in pieces. The cracked glass lenses had both fallen out of the headset and the broken glass was spread out across the floor.

"Alexander! Those glasses are bloody expensive, and the damage will have to be paid for!" Olivia scolded him. It wasn't the first time that one of the members had lost their temper after a mission they had undertaken had not gone to plan, but Alexander had to be one of the worst members to deal with when he made an error.

"I don't give a fuck about how much they cost. Just bill me! Now let's get back to the most important thing, and I won't ask you this question again. What was my overall score?" He demanded. Olivia was no longer in the mood for playing games with him.

"Your score has come back from the other members; they marked your attempt at just fourteen points. It's not the worst score on record, but it is still pathetic. There were points deducted for sloppiness in your execution and a near miss. Worse than that, they marked you down as you were almost seen by a witness!"

"Fourteen? How dare they! Fuck you!" Alexander hollered. He had heard enough, and he stormed out of the clubhouse, slamming every door behind him as he went. As usual, Olivia was left to clean up the mess before the next weekly session would commence.

Brandon straightened his tie as he entered through the front door of the office building. He walked up to the security gate and emptied the contents of his pocket, including his keys, wallet and a handful of loose coins and placed them all into a plastic tray. He moved forward until he was standing under the security tunnel and the metal detection buzzer remained silent.

The security guard in front waved him through. On the other side of the desk, he was requested to sign himself in, and he was asked by the guard who his business was within the offices today. He told the guard that he had been summoned to a meeting with the director of operations, and her office was on the top floor of the building. The guard checked to verify that the meeting with the director was recorded on her schedule, and once this had been confirmed, he allowed him through the second security barrier.

He picked up his possessions from the tray and Brandon placed them back in his trouser pockets, then walked across the hall toward the lifts. After pressing the button to call them down, Brandon waited patiently for one of the lifts to arrive. The right-hand lift must have already been close to the ground floor as the chime sounded to tell him that the lift had reached his level just seconds later. When the doors opened, the lift was empty.

Brandon stepped inside and turned around to face the open doors. He pressed the button numbered thirty on the panel and as the doors closed, the lift started to move and he placed his hands behind his back, with his feet flat on the floor.

The lift ascended at speed and a few seconds later, it juddered to a halt, and slowly the doors opened. Brandon stepped out into the hallway, and the lift doors closed behind him. The thick red carpet on this floor was soft underfoot as he began walking towards the operations room at the other end of the hall. There were two guards posted outside of the door as was usually the case, and Brandon smiled at them both as he continued forward.

The guards did not return his smile. Instead, both guards moved across to block Brandon's path as he approached them, they were prepared to deny him entry. He flashed his identity card and then held both of his hands out to the sides and allowed one of the guards to pat him down and check for any hidden weapons. The guards were changed regularly, and these two burly goons were new to the job.

“Be gentle with me.” Brandon joked, but neither of the guards smiled.

The security procedures may have been over the top, but Samantha was afforded the best protection that money could buy. She had made many enemies over the years, and she didn't care whom she took down within the criminal underworld, and time travel could be a very lucrative business. She was carrying out a promise to her late father that she would clean up the scourge of those who believed that they were above the law. In her experience, the richer the target, the more they thought that they were unstoppable, and how she loved to prove them wrong.

One of the guards punched in his access code in the control panel, and when Samantha was ready, she opened the door from inside with her remote sensor, allowing Brandon to enter the room. He adjusted the cuffs on his shirt and straightened the lapels on his jacket as he stepped inside.

"You called for me," Brandon said. He was surprised to see that Samantha was not alone in her office.

Sitting on the far side of the room, there was a middle-aged man who looked around fifty to sixty years of age. He was wearing the most ridiculous toupee that was badly fitted, and slightly lopsided. Samantha stood up from her desk and walked over towards Brandon, she was carrying a lead crystal glass in her hand. She handed it over to Brandon who smiled before he raised the glass to his nose.

"Now that smells like a good quality Irish single malt. You know me too well." Brandon smiled and then he kissed Samantha on both cheeks one after the other, before taking a small sip of the alcohol and using the next few seconds to appreciate the flavour. "Very smooth." Brandon smiled and he nodded his head in approval.

The man with the dubious toupee stood up from the leather armchair that he had been seated in and limped over towards Brandon with his hand held out in front of him.

"Brandon, this man is Michael Dufray," Samantha said, as Brandon shook the man's hand.

Dufray's grip was weak, and his skin was very smooth. It looked like his nails had been manicured recently too. Brandon made it his business to notice these tiny little details to better understand the person he was dealing with. He took an immediate disliking to Dufray, but he wasn't quite sure why.

"Pleased to meet you at long last Brandon. I have been trying to locate you, and your people, for a very long time. I need to ask you for your help, and in return, I have something in my possession that I know you want.

Samantha began to walk back over toward her desk and chair.

"Why don't you take a seat, Brandon? Mr Dufray has a very interesting story that I think you would love to hear;" Samantha said as she sat down. She was smiling at him.

Brandon took his glass in his hand, and he too sat down on one of the office's two luxurious Italian leather chairs. He edged back on the seat and then sipped a little more of the whiskey. Whatever this man was about to tell him, Samantha had already vetted him thoroughly before he had been allowed into the offices and she took him to be genuine, otherwise, she would never have called Brandon in to hear his story.

Brandon has already assumed that this was going to be a private job, the like of which would come along from time to time. Whenever someone had gone back and made a mess of things, they often needed Brandon to go back and clean up the mess after them. It was just business, but it allowed the timelines to be cleaned up by an expert.

Brandon was an expensive asset for any individual to try and hire privately, but there was a good reason for that. It was because he was the very best at what he did. As Dufray opened his mouth and started to tell his story, Brandon sensed that this man could not be trusted, without knowing the reason why. There was just something very odd, that he could not yet put his finger on, but he would soon work it out for himself.

Rinse and repeat.

After Sharon opened her eyes in fright, she gasped for breath, and the air flooded into her lungs. She sat bolt upright to find herself confused and in unfamiliar surroundings. She could see from a crack in the curtains that outside of the window, the sun was starting to rise in the early morning sky. It must still have been early in the morning, as with the curtains drawn, it was relatively dark in the room.

For a few seconds, Sharon found herself gasping for breath. She placed her hands on her throat and chest to check for injuries, but there were none. Sharon had just experienced a frighteningly real nightmare, and she swore that she could taste blood in her mouth from where her throat had been cut with a razor-sharp blade. It was a nightmare, and nothing more. Slowly, she calmed her breathing down to a regular pace.

After her heartbeat had slowed to its normal rate, she began to recognise her surroundings. Sharon then remembered that she had spent the previous evening here at her friend Debbie's house. She did not recall falling asleep, and her back was now covered in sweat. The last thing that she could remember, was that the pair had been watching movies while enjoying pizza. They had also drunk a few glasses of wine, and the empty glasses were still on the coffee table, along with a few pizza boxes. She checked her watch, and it was just before half past four in the morning.

It felt as if she had experienced this moment in the past and the feeling of Deja vu flooded her thoughts and sent a shiver down her spine. Sharon thought about calling a taxi to take her home but decided against it. She thought that she would probably sicken herself and the driver if they were cooped up in the car along with the smell of her sweaty clothes. She decided that a walk in the early morning air might do her good. Sharon would have used Debbie's bathroom, but it was next to her bedroom, and she did not want to wake her up. Instead, she would take a shower when she reached her home.

It was the middle of June, and the early morning weather was warming up nicely outside already. She thought about leaving a little thank you note on the sofa for when Debbie came down to find her gone, but she had just had a dream about doing this very same thing, and she quickly changed her mind. She wanted things to be as different as possible from her nightmare. It felt as if making some changes helped her feel safer.

After letting herself out of the house as quietly as possible, Sharon closed the door behind her. She knew that the fastest way home was to head down the hill and walk through the town centre, but because she had walked that way in her nightmare, she decided to walk to the bottom of the town and along bridge street instead.

Then she would head right and along junction road, past where the old bingo hall used to be.

As she made her way down the hill, she was passed by a silver Audi car, with a personalised registration plate. The last three letters were KOP. The driver had to be a Liverpool fan, but now Sharon did a double take. She turned and looked at the car again. She felt even more uncomfortable now because she remembered the car's number plate from her nightmare. This felt wrong on so many levels.

The town centre was eerily quiet, aside from the gentle sound of birdsong as the animals gathered on the rooftops. They stared at her as she made her way toward the old town gaol, which was complete with a fake prisoner inside. She thought about turning around and heading back toward Debbie's house, but she had to accept that it was just a nightmare, and there was nothing to be afraid of. She was scaring herself and doing a damn good job of it too.

Sharon turned around as she sensed that she was being followed. She looked all around checking in every direction. She looked to the sides and then behind her, but there was no one anywhere nearby. She sped up and she was almost at jogging speed when she made her way along Bridge Street, crossing over the river Anton. To her right, she could see the old town mills, which had been converted into a pub but had kept the old water wheel in operation. The pub was closed, and she jogged further until she emerged from the other end of the town centre. As she reached the dual carriageway, she ignored the traffic lights crossing button and ran across the road before any early morning traffic came along to slow her down.

After feeling a stitch coming on, Sharon slowed to a walking pace at Junction Road. She caught her breath as she passed the blocks of flats over to her right-hand side. Her home was only about a ten-minute walk from here. She just had to make it past the underpass opposite the old Andover workhouse and her home was just in front of that. Behind her, somewhere in the far distance, some geese had been disturbed by someone, and they were harping away noisily.

The sound of the geese screaming was exactly like she had heard in her nightmare, and it scared her enough that she started to run again. She sprinted half of the way along the road until she was at the old hostel. She looked right when she reached the underpass and was relieved to see that it was empty. There was no one anywhere near her, so she paused and put her hands on her knees while she allowed herself to catch her breath properly.

She was still bent over and drawing in deep breaths as she started laughing to herself. It had just been a stupid nightmare after all, and she had made a complete idiot of herself by getting so worked up about it. She stood up and took the early morning air in as deep as she could and then exhaled it from her lungs. She was still giggling as she started walking the last stretch toward her home which was now less than a few minutes away. Suddenly, she heard something moving out from the large trunked tree that was just behind her.

Beads of sweat formed on Sharon's forehead and as she turned around, there was a loud grunt and in the last seconds of her life, she saw a glint of sunlight glimmering across the blade of a large double-headed axe. The blade moved quickly through the air toward her, and she could not avoid the weapon as it sliced right through her neck, cutting it cleanly from one side to the other.

Sharon stood motionless in time, trying to understand what had just happened. She wanted to run away, but nothing was functioning as it should anymore. Her legs and arms would not respond, and although she could still see, everything was starting to fade to black. Her eyes rolled into the back of her head as a bright blue flash of light illuminated a small area in front of her.

Along junction road, a paperboy was running late, and he fumbled as he unlocked the combination chain on his bike. He took his empty paper bag and threw the strap over his head. He adjusted it so that it was comfortable around his shoulder. The boy placed the lock safely around the crossbar, and then he opened the metal gate at the front of his parent's garden. After pushing his bike out onto the pavement, he closed the gate behind him as quietly as he could. He didn't want Mr Rodgers at number thirty complaining to his parents about the noise he made again.

The boy jumped onto the bike and after sorting his feet out, he started to peddle. He rode left along the road heading towards the town centre. Someone was standing on the path and leaning on the tree by the turn for the underpass. It was probably another drunken reveller, but they were standing right where he needed to turn to take a shortcut through the underpass, otherwise, he would not make it to work on time.

He had regrets about playing video games until two in the morning with his friends now, his parents had told him numerous times to turn it off, but he had just ignored them. He was tired and needed to go back to bed for a few more hours, so he intended to get the papers delivered quickly, and then get home again as fast as he could.

The paperboy rang his bike's bell to warn the pedestrian that he was behind them, but they did not move to the side. He rang it again, thinking that the person might have some headphones in or be hard of hearing, but they remained in the same spot, without moving. As he approached the figure, he could see that it was a female who was leaning on the tree, but there was something odd about her.

As the boy cycled past the female, his paper bag clipped her arm, and the woman's severed head fell to the pavement, spraying blood in all directions as it landed. The boy was horrified, and he slammed on both of his brakes stopping the bike dead in its tracks. Then the headless body fell forward. As it crashed to the floor, blood splattered out from the neck, and sprayed over him. In his terror, the boy could not draw breath. He didn't even feel the stream of warm urine flowing down his trouser leg.

He looked down at his trousers in shame. He was scared out of his wits and as he panicked, he struggled to turn around his bike. As soon as he was facing the direction of his house, he cycled away as fast as he could, no longer caring about his urine-soaked trousers. He wanted to scream, but he didn't dare make a sound, just in case the woman's killer was still close by.

As Mr Dufray edged forward on his chair, Brandon sat back further into his seat and relaxed, it was time for him to listen to this odd man's story.

"What I am about to tell you may seem fantastical, or perhaps it may come across as complete madness. I can assure you that what I am about to disclose to you is true though."

Brandon smiled at Dufray. He had been here listening to amateur time tinkerers too many times before for his liking, all of them filled with regrets for the mess they had made, but he was curious as to what Mr Wonky Toupee was about to tell him.

"You can be assured that what you are about to tell us will be taken seriously, and will remain in our confidence," Samantha assured Dufray.

After taking in a deep breath, Dufray cleared his throat noisily by coughing into his hand before he continued.

"Just over a year ago, I sold my business portfolio for slightly over one and a half a billion pounds. I suddenly had more money than I knew what to do with." Dufray had now started to attract Brandon's attention. "I retired from business life before I had reached the age of thirty."

Had he heard that right? Brandon was feeling somewhat confused. He examined Dufray's face a little more closely, and even from the far side of the room, he could see that the man was well past the age of thirty, so something wasn't quite adding up with his story.

"I found myself with a lot of time on my hands, so I travelled the world seeking out new thrills to try. I discovered that the activities I used to love were becoming less and less enjoyable, so I took up big game hunting for sport, which I found quite exhilarating."

Brandon felt his inner rage rising rapidly, and he could not control his anger.

"How very brave of you. To go out in the wild protected by armed guides while shooting down endangered defenceless creatures." Brandon sneered at him. He hated seeing animals treated cruelly.

"Have you ever watched a large predator die?"

"It's not something that I would find entertaining."

"It is the most intense feeling you can ever have. I consider it comparable to being a God." Dufray looked quite pleased with himself. "You see when the animal is about to draw its final breath, no matter how large the animal is, fear fills its eyes. No creature wants to die as they all fear the unknown. They know that they are dying, and even though you could have let them live, you have chosen to end them for pleasure. That is what Gods do, they kill indiscriminately."

"You're not a God Dufray, you are just a sick and twisted rich old man who needs teaching a lesson."

Brandon's fists were clenched tightly, and Dufray noticed that his knuckles were red, so he decided to try and calm the situation down between the two of them.

"Please, I understand your anger at what I used to do and I'm not proud of the things I've done, but you haven't heard the worst bit of the story yet, so please reserve your judgement of me until then." Brandon didn't like the sound of that, but Samantha was glaring at him, and it was obvious that she was unimpressed with his last outburst.

Sensing Samantha's annoyance with him, Brandon bit his tongue and allowed Dufray to continue.

"Through my association with other friends who also hunted game, I was eventually introduced to a man who went by the name of Alexander Berg. He is part of an elite collective of rich socialites and one of the recruitment agents for a group that he called 'The Perfect Kill Club.' He promised me that they could offer me an experience unlike anything else in the entire world.

I was curious and excited as he asked me if I wanted to join them and feel the thrill for myself. Three of my hunting friends were already members of the club, and they were keen that I joined them. The price of membership for joining this elitist and ultra-secret club was a paltry ten million pounds."

Before Dufray continued, he paused for a few seconds, and stared at the ceiling, as if he had forgotten what he was about to say. Then a smile came across his face, as it came back to him.

"I wish that I could tell you that I thought long and hard about joining the club, but I agreed to participate there and then. When you have so much money and nothing but time on your hands, you consider a sum like that as just a small price to pay for the promise of an experience that was sold to me, as the thrill of a lifetime.

After I had paid the membership fee, Alexander told me to be ready at a moment's notice. The following day I had a call from my reception team, to tell me that a car was waiting for me outside of the gates of my house. I dressed and then went down to find a limo waiting for me, and the door was open, so I climbed inside.

I was asked to wear a dark hood so that I could be driven to a secret location, to which I agreed. When we arrived at the clubhouse, I was walked inside by two fellow members, then my hood was removed. During my time there, I was utterly amazed at what I saw." Dufray felt his mind drifting back to that fateful day that would change his life forever.

In The Club.

As the chair of the meeting removed the hood from his head, Dufray's blinked rapidly as his eyes took a few seconds to adjust to the light of the room. When his eyes had focused, he recognised some of the faces who were sitting in a semi-circle within the large room. The assembled guests were all staring at him with glee.

"Welcome to the club." The chair said, and the nineteen members who were present, all stood in unison and gave Dufray a rapturous round of applause.

The chair of the club was a former high-ranking politician. Among the faces that were present, Dufray recognised an actor and a female pop star. He knew some of the others too, but he couldn't put names to any of the other faces.

"Take a seat and let us demonstrate what we do in the club, and then if you think that you are ready, you can experience the thrill of the kill for yourself," Alexander told him.

The other members all sat down hurriedly in readiness for the game to begin. Dufray sat down in an empty chair which he assumed correctly, was his. When the members all signalled that they were ready, a large screen was activated, and what looked like an old broadcast from a news programme was paused on the screen. The lights within the room became dim and there was a palpable buzz of excitement among the members.

Alexander pressed the play button on the remote control to begin the playback. The reporter's voice bellowed through tiny but powerful speakers which filled the room with sound.

"Police are still calling for witnesses to the brutal slaying of nineteen-year-old Sharon Tasker. The young woman was callously murdered early on Monday morning of this week. Reports say that she was repeatedly stabbed in the face, in what police have described as a particularly brutal and vicious attack.

The woman was subjected to a frenzied ordeal, and she was reported to have suffered over thirty stab wounds to the face and skull. Police and ambulance crews both attended, but she was pronounced dead at the scene. The Police are still unsure as to any motive for the attack and are asking for anyone who may have seen her walking in the area, or who may have C.C.T.V. or dash-cam footage to come forward." The video was then paused, and the news clip was returned to the starting point.

This was a little disturbing to Dufray, who felt a little out of his depth.

"I don't quite understand. What's going on here?" Dufray whispered to the man who was sitting over to his left.

"Don't worry, just sit back and enjoy the ride. I was the same at first. Just watch what happens on the screen. Everything will soon become clear." He was smiling. "Everyone else was just as confused as you are at the start of the game."

A woman stood up and addressed the members who were present in the hall.

"For those of you who don't know me, my name is Olivia, and I am the controller of the game. Under your seats, we have placed electronic score pads. All individual scores that you give are anonymous and confidential. Now, before we can begin, let us all move over to the chamber in the next room, and then we can decide on who goes back next."

Everyone seemed excited. They all stood up in unison. Some were chatting loudly, while others were laughing as they moved in single file towards the rear of the hall. As they entered the next room, there was a large cylindrical transparent tube inside. It stood around eight feet tall and just over two feet in diameter. It was on a platform that slightly elevated it from the floor.

Olivia was standing alone over on the far side of the room. She was standing ready to activate what looked like some kind of touch screen device.

"Good luck everyone," Olivia said, without turning around.

Every person in the room stood in silence in eager anticipation of the result. “Today’s winner is..” Everyone in attendance was waiting with bated breath to hear the name of the winner announced. The excitement was building, and some members of the group started to chant the word ‘Kill’ repeatedly.

As the excitement reached a fever pitch, Olivia pressed the generator button on her tablet. The app began its random selection, and once the name was generated, she turned around and held the tablet aloft, displaying the lucky winner’s name for the group to see.

There were one or two groans as the outcome was revealed. It seemed as if this winner had more than his fair share of winning the weekly draw.

“The winner is Alexander again! You lucky thing. Congratulations!” She smiled, and Alexander moved through the gathered members, most of whom cheered him on, slapping his back as he headed over towards the cylinder.

Alexander kissed Olivia on both of her cheeks. He looked elated to have been chosen yet again. He seemed to be luckier than most as of late, but Olivia had often assured the members that the selection was completely random. Olivia moved over to the left of the machine and opened up the doors to a huge cupboard. Inside the cupboard was a variety of different weapons in every different shape and size imaginable.

"Alexander, please select your weapon in readiness for the hunt," Olivia told him as she moved back over to the control panel ready to activate the machine.

"This time, I choose.. the Double-headed battle axe." Immediately, another member removed it from the hooks and carried it over to where Alexander was standing in readiness to play.

He moved the axe from one hand to the other becoming accustomed to the weight of the weapon as he swung it in the air. It felt good and sturdy in his hands. It would be perfect for the mission he imagined.

"You may now enter into the chamber Alexander," Olivia announced. The control panel had automatically adjusted the settings to account for the weapon, and now there was an air of excitement building again among the other members as they waited for the game to start.

Alexander gripped the axe in his hands and watched in silence as the glass cylinder slid open. He stood patiently waiting in front of the tube for his mission to begin.

"Are you ready to play the game?" Olivia asked him.

"I am ready."

"Then repeat the rules of the game before I execute the command," Olivia requested. It was a chore to have to repeat the rules every time that each participant played the game, but they were a necessary evil.

“There will be no interaction with anyone other than the intended target. Scores will only count if an original ending occurs. Beware of the butterfly effect. Leave immediately once the task is completed, without taking any souvenirs of the visit.” The rules were self-explanatory.

“May your score be an improvement on the last one,” Olivia said, with a wide smile. History was about to be made yet again.

Alexander stepped into the machine and as he turned around the door of the machine began to close over him. He placed one hand around the axe, and the other onto a holding handle fixed to the wall. Alexander smiled and closed his eyes tightly as he waited for the tingle of the plasma flood that would surround his body, to occur.

Olivia activated the switch on the control panel and the countdown timer started at the number five and descended to zero.

“You have fifteen minutes before the reset. Happy hunting, and may your kill be an original one!” She shouted at him, unsure if he could still hear her from inside of the machine.

A brilliant bright blue light filled the room as an electrical charge burst through the cylinder. Alexander arched his back as the charge spread through the plasma in the chamber. His adventure was just about to begin. Within seconds, the light grew brighter and then as if by magic, he was gone from the chamber. He had less than a quarter of an hour to complete the task, and this time he was determined to do better.

A New Flame

The remaining members walked back into the first room and Dufray followed close behind. He watched as they picked up the electronic score pads placed under each of the seats, and then he collected and examined his score pad. The members were all sitting down in front of the large screen again, and a selection of drinks and snacks was served to everyone. The face of the same presenter was paused on the screen, ready to deliver his broadcast once again.

Dufray was still confused about what was happening, but he remained silent with the scorepad in his hands and just watched on patiently. Olivia waited until everyone was settled and then she spoke to the members.

"We have a new recruit with us here today who is sadly ineligible to vote on this round, but for his benefit, I need to explain the rules surrounding the scoring system of the game. The kills are scored across four sections. Ruthlessness, speed, efficiency and originality. Each is scored between zero and three. Three is the top score available in each category.

If every eligible member present selects the maximum of four points, then the prize will be awarded for the perfect kill." When fifteen minutes had passed, Olivia pressed play on the remote and the presenter started to relay the news story to the assembled club members as if for the first time.

“The Police are still calling for witnesses to the brutal slaying of nineteen-year-old Sharon Tasker. The young woman was brutally murdered in the early hours of Monday morning this week in what police have described as a truly vicious and barbaric act’. The woman was discovered by a paperboy, who was cycling to his place of work to collect the morning papers.

Horrifically, from the boy’s statement, it appears that the woman had been decapitated with a razor-sharp weapon which is believed to have been a replica medieval-style double-headed axe. Police are still unsure as to any motive for the attack and are asking for anyone else who may have seen the victim walking in the area, or who may have dash-cam footage of the woman making her way home, to come forward urgently.”

Olivia stood up and paused the news segment with her remote control. If Dufray had felt confused before, now he was completely bewildered. Olivia then retracted the screen before she addressed the members again.

“Could I ask you to input your scores into the devices now please?” She requested, and each of the members started pressing buttons on the pads. The scores were then uploaded to the central computer where only Olivia could see the result.

The Return

Bright blue lights flashed inside the cylinder and Alexander reappeared inside the machine. His face, hands and clothing were all covered in blood. He released the axe and it fell to the floor of the chamber. He was smiling as the cylinder opened, and it was clear that he felt more confident about achieving a better score after last week's fiasco.

"That kill was so much better and far cleaner than last time," Olivia told him.

"Well, don't keep me waiting. What was the score?" He asked excitedly. Olivia preferred him when he was in this mood.

"Your score was twenty-seven, one of the highest scores this quarter. It was a clean and quick kill, and you ported out before there was any chance that you could be seen by the boy. It was very efficiently done!" She praised him.

"That's great, but I was still hoping for a slightly better score than that. Never mind."

Alexander returned the axe for cleaning before it could be returned to the weapons store, and then he walked out of the room and into the member's chamber to a rapturous round of applause. The members were slapping him on the back or shaking his bloodstained hands. Dufray looked shocked as Alexander approached him.

“That is how it’s done, my boy. Next week, it’s your turn.” Dufray shook his head, feeling more confused than ever at what he had just seen.

Regrets, I've had a few.

Dufray could remember that moment as clear as if it were yesterday. Suddenly he broke down in tears in his chair. Samantha walked across the room, and she held out a box of tissues. He took one out of the box and wiped his eyes dry, then he placed it in his trouser pocket.

"I'm sorry, but that moment changed my life forever," Dufray said quietly as he slowly began to regain his composure until he was ready to continue with his story.

"I'm confused. Are you saying that they are using time travel to go back and murder people?" Brandon asked, thinking that Dufray might have some type of mental illness or that he was fantasizing. Any such event in the past would have caused ripples in time that they would have detected by now.

"Not people. They have targeted just one girl. They have been going back time after time to commit cold-blooded murder to the same person." Dufray replied.

"Well, that is some story, but if you would excuse me. I don't have time to entertain this fantasy." Brandon stood up from his chair. He had heard enough of this man's delusions and he was ready to leave.

"Wait," Samantha said. "I wouldn't have called you in if I didn't think that we needed you. Please listen to the rest of the story. Just hear him out." Her eyes were pleading with him to remain.

Brandon looked at Samantha and he shook his head in disbelief. Then he sat back down reluctantly, waiting to hear the rest of this deluded man's story.

"Did you know that time travel was almost perfected by the Nazis back in the nineteen forties? The unfinished time technology was confiscated by the Americans after the second world war ended. Knowledge of the equipment needed to travel through time has been suppressed from the general public.

Over the last thirty years, I have come to know all about your secret organisation, and how you were tasked with destroying all the time machines, but I can assure you that your mission is incomplete and I know that two time machines are still in existence. I know they exist because I have one of them in my possession.

Nikola Tesla invented a safe way to travel in time and he foolishly shared some of his ideas with the government, but he did not trust them, so he held back a little and wisely decided not to share everything. He had the complete designs for a fully functioning machine. He handed the full designs over to a naval officer just before his death. The officer was supposed to use the machine for the good of mankind and to correct any mistakes the government made.

The officer tasked an engineer with creating the time machine from Tesla's plans, but after he discovered what he had at his disposal, unknown to the officer, he made a replica, and secretly sold it to the highest bidder."

Brandon looked as if he was becoming a little angry. He and all his fellow officers had spent a very long time trying to make sure that all the time devices had been destroyed, and now with the confirmation that Tesla's machines existed, he knew that he still had work to do. He needed to locate both machines and destroy them, but he did not trust Dufray to be a man of his word.

Brandon would have to be smart about how he approached this mission, to ensure its success. A question popped into his head.

"If what you have told us is true, the club is still operating and the members are jumping back to make changes in the past, then our futures would have been changed. The timelines would have rippled and there would be evidence of them being broken. These events would still register no matter how small, so why haven't we detected them?" Brandon was all too aware of the time ripples caused by the butterfly effect.

"I assure you that they have been going back, but only to kill one person whose death will make no difference to the future timelines. This is the beauty of their plan, as they know that her death will not register. Tell me, have you ever had a dream that you thought was real? Or lived through a moment that you had experienced before, but expected a different outcome?" Brandon had to admit that the answer to both of these questions was yes, and he nodded his head.

"I have."

"Or an odd feeling of Deja vu maybe, just as another example. Subtle little changes in the timeline occur, but some still retain memories of the old timeline. They call it 'The Mandela effect.' Have you heard of that?"

"Yes." Brandon had heard of it, but he was still curious to know where this story was now heading.

"Then you know that the Mandela effect is where large numbers of people remember something that most others say never happened. Some say that Nelson Mandela had never made it out of prison alive. They remember the news of his death being televised in the nineteen-eighties. Lots of people share that same memory and there are numerous other examples recorded like this."

"Ok. Let's say that I believe you. Then why would they be going back in time to murder this young woman?"

"This is why I called you in, this is the point where it gets a little bit more interesting," Samantha interjected.

“They are sadistic bastards, whose only reason for slaughtering an innocent, is that they are using her in a sick game to try and achieve a ‘perfect’ score. As I told you, history records that the woman dies anyway. She was hit by a drunk driver who had no idea of what he had done and had fled from the scene. The woman died instantly from a severe head injury.”

“I don't understand, what is it that you are trying to tell me?” Brandon was only getting a small part of what was happening here.

“In simple terms, they know that the girl dies so they can go back to the moment before her death and murder her over and over again. It changes nothing in the future as they never found the motorist who ran her down. They score the member’s kill method from the changes to the news report, and the objective for the club members is to achieve the perfect kill score. They can only achieve this if they are awarded top marks from everyone in the club.”

“Assuming that I believe all this to be true. What is it that you want from me?” Brandon asked him.

“I want you to go back in time to just before the event, and I want to go with you to prevent them from doing this to me.” He then stood up from his chair.

Dufray removed the toupee from his head, and Brandon realised why it looked so out of place. Part of Dufray’s head was missing. His skull was covered in scars, and for the first time, Brandon could see that Dufray had a false eye hidden underneath his fake hair as well.

"What the hell happened to you?" Brandon asked him.

"I failed on my first attempt. I fucked everything up."

Dufray sighed heavily he thought back to the moment of his first jump, and he was ready to tell Brandon what happened when he went back in time to try and murder the woman for himself.

Crisis point

It was twenty-four hours before Dufray's first-time jump, and he had spent the best part of the day learning the history of time travel, and the strict rules associated with going back in time. He was given a device to fasten around his wrist that allowed him to activate an emergency return. It was stressed to him over and over again that he had to take the utmost care not to change anything in the past and the seriousness of potentially altering the future.

It all felt unreal like he was a character in a science fiction film. When he returned the following day, he felt nervous, but he was determined to make the jump and experience the thrill of the kill for himself. He gave no thought to the suffering of the woman; he was quickly becoming besotted by the idea of committing murder and getting away with it. He wanted to be the first member to achieve the perfect kill.

The gathered members applauded as Dufray stepped into the chamber room. Olivia smiled at him and then she opened the weapon cupboard doors.

"Dufray, as a new member, you have the pleasure of today's first scheduled jump. Now, please select your weapon for the kill," Olivia told him as she moved away from the cupboard and walked over to the control console, ready to set the machine. Dufray examined the vast array of weapons on offer.

“I choose. I choose the colt 45.” Dufray said. A fellow member removed the gun from its hook and checked it over carefully to ensure that the weapon was fully loaded. She handed it over to Dufrey. It was a lot heavier than he expected it to be.

“Are you positive about your choice of weapon?” Olivia asked him.

“Yes, I am sure.” He assured her.

“Then you may now step forward and enter the chamber,” Olivia said. The gathered members all watched on excitedly. The glass cylinder was locked in an open position and Dufray was breathing heavily as he stood in front of the tube. He felt a little sick at the thought of what he was about to do, but everyone assured him that statistically, time travel was safer than walking across the road.

“Before I jump, can I just ask, what happens if I mess this up? Will I still get another go?”

“Don’t worry. If things don’t go to plan, we have a way to fix every eventuality.” Olivia reassured him, and she smiled across at Alexander.

“Right, I think that I am ready now.” Dufray had felt comforted by her response.

"Now, I need you to repeat the rules before I execute the jump command," Olivia instructed. Dufray had already practised his response many times over.

"I should have no interaction with anyone other than the intended target. The scores only count if there is an original kill. I should be wary of the butterfly effect, and erm... oh yes, I should leave once the task is completed, without taking any souvenirs of the visit." He was happy to have remembered the rules.

"May your first score be a good one," Olivia told him in all sincerity.

Dufray took a deep breath before walking into the machine and as he turned to face Olivia, the door closed over the top of the chamber. For a few seconds, Dufray thought about pressing the emergency door release and aborting the mission, but a big part of him wanted to know how it felt to go back in time. He was desperate to try and murder a human being, and experience the thrill for himself.

Olivia activated the switch and the countdown timer which appeared to be descending in slow motion as it moved from five to zero.

"You have fifteen minutes to complete the kill before the reset. Now go and blow that bitch away." Dufray smiled, but he was breathing heavily, and his heart was racing in his chest.

Dufray screamed in panic as a thin layer of plasma covered his skin, and it tingled. It was too late to abort the mission now. The same bright blue lights filled the chamber and his journey into the past had begun. The members of the club were laughing and jeering loudly at his reactions inside of the tube. All of them could remember the first time that they had jumped back through time, and they too had felt the same fear of the unknown.

Dufray felt disorientated as his body silently materialised out of thin air. He appeared in the exact spot by the side of the underpass where he was shown that he would land. He tucked the gun safely into his trousers away from view and started to make his way to where he would make his encounter with the woman, and then he was going to experience the thrill of hunting down and executing a human for the very first time.

You don't need a gun.

As Sharon woke up, she realised that she had fallen asleep on Debbie's sofa, and she felt uncomfortably hot. Debbie had covered her up with her spare duvet, but she didn't need a cover in this heat. Sharon looked at the clock on the wall and it was just after half past four in the morning. Her neck felt stiff as if she had slept awkwardly. It was hardly surprising after spending a night with her head propped at an odd angle on the arm of the sofa.

It was the middle of June, and the early morning weather looked to be warm outside so Sharon decided to walk home rather than try to get a taxi at this hour. She found a pen and paper and scribbled out a little thank you note on the sofa for when Debbie woke up, and then she let herself out of the house as quietly as possible. She walked down the hill and continued through the town, passing through the unlocked portion of the Andover town's Chantry Centre and then she would turn down towards the college.

As she made her way down the hill, a silver Audi passed her, and she turned back to look at the number plate which read KOP. She felt a shiver running down her spine as if someone had just walked over her grave. She made her way through the town centre and then took a shortcut through the leisure centre. She was passed by the occasional car but there were very few other people awake at this time in the morning.

As she turned the corner by the leisure centre, she encountered a flock of Canadian geese who squawked at her noisily in unison and made her jump. The birds were far enough away from her, that she was able to jog around them and avoid having to cut through the middle of the noisy animals. Now she just had to walk through the underpass and that path would bring her out to the site of the old Andover workhouse, and her home was just to the right of that.

Behind her, the geese were still harping noisily, and Sharon laughed to herself at how the birds had frightened the life out of her. They were big birds, but they were just geese after all. As she walked into the shadows beneath the underpass, she noticed that a man was walking down the path, heading straight toward her. He removed something from his trousers and was holding it in his hand. It looked like he was pointing it straight at her head. Nothing about this scenario made any sense to her at all.

A shot rang out and a piece of wall came away in the underpass. Sharon realised to her horror, that the stranger had a gun in his hand, as he took another shot at her. In fear of her life, Sharon ran back toward the college and Dufray took yet another shot which grazed her right arm. She screamed out loud in pain but continued to run despite her wound. Sharon was determined to get away from her attacker at any cost.

She ran across the grassy hill over to her left and then up the path toward the dual carriageway. She was hoping to see a car that she could flag down for help, but she was disappointed, though not surprised to see that the road was empty in both directions. The people of Andover were still sleeping while she was running for her life.

A fourth shot rang out from behind, as the man continued to chase her. With Sharon running away so fast, it was difficult for Dufray to chase her and get a decent shot off at the same time. In the houses directly in front of Sharon, a light came on in one of the bedrooms, and a man opened the window to see what all the fuss was about. He was ready to tear someone a new arsehole for waking him up so early in the morning.

At the last second. Sharon spotted the shirtless man who was now leaning out of the window, and she screamed at him in a panic.

"Help me, he's trying to kill me!" She pleaded. The man looked straight at her, then he popped his head back inside, closed the window and disappeared. "You bastard! You are a fucking coward|!" Sharon screamed out to him in her frustration.

Unknown to Sharon the shirtless man was making an emergency call to the police at that very moment. She looked over her shoulder to see that the man with the gun was still chasing after her, but she was much faster and slowly she was managing to distance herself from him. She sprinted for the path on the other side of the road that would take her back to the underpass.

The man behind was slowing up even more. Sharon just had to turn right after the tunnel, and she would be able to make it back to the safety of her home. She was growing more confident by the second, that she was going to survive this ordeal, and she was hopeful that she would see this man brought to justice.

Sharon turned the corner at speed, looking back over her shoulder to gauge the growing distance between her and the attacker. She screamed as she turned around and ran straight into the chest of a large blonde-haired man who had come from nowhere.

"Hey, hey take it easy." The blonde man said as he held her by the top of her arms.

"Help me! He's trying to kill me!" She pleaded, and the man smiled at her before slicing deep across her throat with a sharp hunting knife in a single swift action.

Sharon fell to the floor while holding her throat to try and stop the blood from flowing. She would be dead before anyone came to her aid. Dufray finally turned the corner, panting heavily. He was too out of shape for running after the girl, even though it had been just a short distance.

“Thank God it’s you, Alexander. I’m so sorry that I screwed this up. I tried to shoot her, but I missed her a few times. Slippery little bitch almost got away.” Dufray apologised.

“It’s okay my friend. Don't worry. Just hand me the gun and then we can sort out all this mess.” Dufray smiled as he handed the weapon straight over to him without giving it a second thought.

Alexander raised the weapon and before Dufray could plead for his life, shot Dufray in the right-hand side of his forehead without hesitation, and Dufray dropped to the floor where his body lay motionless.

“You are a fucking pathetic idiot!” Alexander shouted, down at Dufray as he wiped the weapons clean.

He placed the gun in one of Dufray’s hands and the hunting knife in one of his jacket pockets.

“Sixty seconds to complete the mission before the interruption. Emergency services are being despatched. You must initiate a return immediately.” The warning alarm on Alexander’s wrist sounded.

He could hear sirens blaring in the distance as the police sped toward the area. Alexander removed the return device from Dufray's wrist. The mess Dufray had created, had been corrected. It was as good a job as he or anyone else could have done here anyway. Olivia was right about Dufray. He was not of a good enough calibre to add to their ranks.

Olivia had an uncanny knack for knowing when new members were likely to fail on a maiden mission. She said that they should never have let him into the club in the first place. Dufray had proven himself to be a total fuck up, and he had nearly ruined everything, but it was a lesson learned that would not be repeated.

"The fatal blow has now been executed, and the target is terminated. You may now activate the return." The device instructed.

The armed police unit sped along the dual carriageway, trying to locate the armed suspect, just as Alexander hit the button on his watch, there was the familiar bright flash of blue light that surrounded him as the thin layer of plasma around his body became activated, and then he was gone. The crime scene was set, and the police would have every reason to think that Dufray had used the knife to kill the girl, and then he had turned the gun on himself.

Sharon lay on the cold concrete slab, and she could feel the blood gushing out from the wound in her neck. Her life was ebbing away quickly. A teenage boy turned down toward the underpass, he was riding on his bike.

The boy had a paper bag hung over his shoulder, and he stopped dead as he noticed the bloody mess on the floor. Sharon was no longer moving, but the man with the injured head opened his left eye. He was too weak to raise his hand.

“Fuck.” The boy said before cycling away towards his parent's house to try and get some help. As he sped around the corner, he spotted the armed policemen and he sped toward them instead of heading home. The boy quickly directed them toward where the injured man and woman lay.

Back to life.

Brandon had to admit, that Dufray's tale was one of the most impressive stories he had ever heard, but it had too many flaws for it to be true.

"So, you are trying to tell me that you survived being shot in the head by a Colt 45 at close range? That sounds like a lucky escape to me." He told Dufray.

"Lucky? You call this fucking lucky?" He shouted.

Dufray was back on his feet. He hobbled across the room with a pronounced limp, and he showed Brandon the scars that covered the entire left-hand side of his head.

"Sit down Mr Dufray! If you still want our help, then might I suggest that you don't antagonise our top agent any further!" Samantha knew that Brandon would react soon if she didn't try to intervene.

"I meant no disrespect. I just meant you were lucky to be alive." Brandon added. He was still looking at the scars all over one side of Dufray's skull. He looked like he had been through numerous operations to try and rebuild his head, but it still looked like a complete mess.

Dufray sneered at Brandon angrily, and then he limped back over to his seat.

“I suffered from partial paralysis. I also had complete memory loss for just over ten years. The real kick in the teeth, was my incarceration for fifteen years for a murder that I did not commit, despite my best efforts to try and shoot her.”

“They thought that you killed her anyway?” Samantha asked.

“Yes, thanks to that bastard Alexander. He was the one who put the gun in my hand and the knife in my pocket. She was dead, and by framing me for the murder, I was as good as dead too.”

“Karma,” Brandon said under his breath. “Something is troubling me. Why didn’t they come back to finish you off?” Brandon asked. He assumed that it would have been high on the club’s agenda to cover all their tracks.

As he sat down again, Dufrey looked distant.

“No one knew who I was. They assumed that I had been trying to kill the girl because I was mentally unstable. I tried to kill myself after and I failed, but the public didn’t need to know that, so it was kept out of the press. I was taken to a secure hospital and my fingerprints were not on file.

As time passed by, I began to have flashbacks and then I started to remember my future from my past. It was only after my release that I discovered everything else that happened through hypnosis sessions with a trusted aide.

I have waited thirty years for this moment, but now I am ready to have my revenge on those who did this to me."

"And just how are you going to exact that?" Brandon asked him.

"I have spent the last ten years planning for this moment, I have used my knowledge of the future to accumulate more wealth than you could ever imagine. I found out the name of the engineer who sold the replica time travel tube and I managed to buy the machine by making the owner an offer that they could not refuse. While searching to try and find the machine, I discovered all about your agency. I wanted to know if you could help.

Money can often open doors that are closed to all others. Now I want to pay you to go back with me and to stop Alexander from shooting me. Then, I will kill him myself for persuading me to join his death club. For leaving me to spend fifteen years being abused in prison, and for coming back and trying to murder me."

Brandon stood up from his chair.

"Thank you for the offer, but I'm not interested in helping you play out this vendetta. We will locate these machines and destroy them; I can assure you of that." He started to button up his jacket before heading towards the exit door. Samantha knew that it was futile to try and change his mind. All she wanted to know, was the whereabouts of both machines.

Dufray started laughing, and Brandon stopped dead. He felt a rage growing inside of him.

"It doesn't matter to me. I will never disclose the locations of the machines until this is finished. The girl always dies anyway so it doesn't matter who goes back and helps me to kill him. The job will get done regardless. Ten million pounds for a few minutes of work is an offer that not many other former agents will be able to refuse."

Brandon knew that Dufray was correct. The agents were pretty much redundant and Dufray had wealth beyond imagination. He would never divulge the whereabouts of the machines, and it wouldn't take long before someone accepted his generous offer. Brandon didn't care about the money, he couldn't help but think about the poor girl who was being murdered time after time solely to provide entertainment for the rich.

Brandon stood in the same spot pondering his response.

"I will do it, but only on one condition," Brandon said, with his back to Dufray.

"Name it."

"After this is done, both of the machines are turned over to our agency to be destroyed." Dufray pondered his proposal for a few seconds.

“Agreed,” Dufray said eventually. It was just what Brandon expected, he knew a liar when he saw one.

“I don’t want your money either. I just want your word on it.”

“I promise you, that you have it,” Dufray said. Brandon didn't trust him to hand over his machine, but whatever happened next, he was sure that this would be an interesting assignment.

The morning after.

As the men parted, Dufray had told him that there was no rush for them to complete the task, as long as it was within the next month. Brandon had asked to be given just seven days to complete the mission and he had requested a trial run before undergoing the rescue attempt. Dufray asked if Brandon could collect him the following morning in his car, and he agreed to do so.

Although Brandon had no love for Dufray, he wanted to know more about this man and what had driven him to do the things that he had done in his life, in case he had judged him harshly. Brandon followed the sat nav until he pulled up at the address he had been given. Dufray came limping out of a hotel on the other side of the road.

It may as well have been winter, as when Dufray left the hotel, he was wearing a hat, and the collar of his coat was turned up. He had a scarf wrapped around his face too. It would be impossible for anyone to recognise him. He tapped on the passenger window while Brandon was looking the other way, and it made Brandon jump in his seat. Dufray peered into the window and Brandon unlocked the car.

Dufray climbed into the passenger seat. He handed Brandon a small piece of paper with a postcode on it.

“Drive me to the area written on here.” He told Brandon abruptly.

After punching the new postcode into the sat nav screen, Brandon checked the mirrors and then he pulled the car out onto the main road, as soon as there was a gap in the busy traffic.

“Where is it that are we heading to?” Brandon asked. He did not recognise the postcode.

“I am going to show you the location of the headquarters of the club. The place where they operate from.”

“Isn’t that a little dangerous? What if they see you?” Brandon asked. It seemed sensible questions to ask.

“They haven't seen me for a very long time. Not since Alexander left me for dead. Thirty years is time enough for nature to disguise my face. We aren't going to get too close to them though. I just want to show you where they keep their machine, ready for when you destroy it and to stop them from going back to change anything else once this is done.”

The pair drove for almost twenty miles before they reached a large property on the right-hand side that was surrounded by a large wall and some heavy wrought iron security gates.

"Keep on driving past the wall. Head straight past the property. This is the place that they call the clubhouse." Dufray said. He looked ready to explode in anger.

"The house looks well protected."

"It is difficult to access unless you know the security code for the gate. The code is six seven six six. Then enter. Easy enough to remember?"

"Sure." It would be hard for Brandon to forget such a simple passcode.

"It is changed regularly, but next Sunday the random number generator they use will change it, and I will have to find out what it has been changed to. I have someone on the inside who happily feeds me information in return for large donations of cash." Brandon pressed the screen on the sat nav and tapped the button to save the postcode in the favourites section.

"Where to now?" Brandon asked him.

"Follow the road for a quarter of a mile then turn right. It's the first turn on the left after that."

Brandon followed the directions he had been given, and within a few minutes, they took a right turn and drove up a steep hill. The next left took them down to a secure isolated industrial unit, away from the main road.

"Here we are," Dufray told him, and Brandon drove the car up to the door and parked the car outside of the unit.

As he stepped out of the car, Brandon could see clearly across the field behind him. There was a clear view of the house that they had just visited. It was at the perfect vantage point which would allow Dufray to spy on the clubhouse.

“Don't you think this place is a little bit too close for comfort?” Brandon asked.

“My late father always told me, keep your friends close, and keep your enemies closer. Right here, this is where I can see them, and I can track all their movements.” Dufray replied. “Come with me.”

He walked over to the building, unlocked the front door to the unit and both men walked inside. Dufray then locked the door behind them for security and to keep out any curious visitors. As they walked further into the unit, Dufray turned the lights on, and inside of the building, it looked like a normal mechanics workshop. There was an old Ford car inside that had been suspended on hydraulic ramps.

Dufray took a key from his chain and turned the power on inside the building. He used a pad to raise the ramps until the car was high enough in the air, that both men were able to walk underneath it.

“This is just a front for prying eyes and to satisfy any nosey neighbours. To see the machine, we need to go downstairs," Dufray said, and he knelt underneath the car and unlocked a padlock on another metal door.

The hidden door was an accessway to a set of stairs leading down to a secret basement. Brandon descended the stairs behind Dufray. He watched Dufray carefully as he unlocked yet another door and then entered the room ahead of him. As he walked in behind Dufray, the time machine was placed centrally in the basement, and it looked vast. It was the first time that Brandon had seen this unusual-looking time tunnel design first-hand. It was a work of art, worthy of a genius like Tesla.

The machine was glimmering, and it looked to be made mostly of glass and metal. It stood on an elevated platform, but even without this step, it looked like it was a good eight feet in height.

"Are you ready for your test run yet?" Dufray asked him.

"Why not." came Brandon's reply, which took Dufray a little off guard.

Brandon was still unsure about this man's story, and how much of it was genuine, but there was only one way for him to find out if his story was true and if these machines worked, he would have to test it out for himself. "I want you to send me back close enough so that I can see what they are doing to the girl for myself." Brandon had a plan forming in his head, but he needed to see the area around where the murder took place.

"I can get you close, but you must promise me that you will not interfere. I want to witness his death, and the girl must die to keep the timeframe stable." Dufray warned.

"You don't need to lecture me. I already know. Trust me, I just want to see a member of this club in action." Brandon could not believe how depraved the idea of this club was. He needed to see it with his own eyes.

Dufray placed a watch-like device on Brandon's wrist before he gave him instructions on its operation.

"Hit the top bottom and hold it for three seconds to activate the return," Dufray instructed. Brandon adjusted the strap, while Dufray spent the next few minutes on the control panel settings the parameters of the jump.

When the calculations were complete, Dufray turned around to face Brandon.

"I am going to send you into an empty flat that is directly opposite the underpass. From there, you will have a clear view of the assassination. I will send you back five minutes before the event so that you can make yourself comfortable." Dufray nodded toward Brandon to let him know that he was ready. "Step into the chamber," Dufray told him.

He walked over to the chamber and stepped inside. Brandon turned around to face Dufray and took a deep breath. This style of the machine was unfamiliar to him. It was nothing like any of the designs he had travelled in before. There was a loud clunk from above his head as two pistons fired and the seal descended until it reached the bottom, and the vacuum seals engaged. A thin layer of plasma surrounded Brandon's body, and it felt like his skin was tingling all over. Then the blue lights from the power flowed through the plasma and lit up the room, and within a few seconds, Brandon was gone.

Pain seared through Sharon's lungs. She had run most of the way home. She regretted spending the night on Debbie's sofa, as she had suffered the worst nightmare imaginable while she slept. Her body hurt in different places, but for no apparent reason. It felt as if she had spent a full twelve rounds in a boxing ring with a heavyweight boxer, and her body had been pummelled relentlessly.

The nightmare had frightened her out of her wits, and she woke up in floods of tears. The nightmare had felt so real, and as she made her way towards the town, every little thing was scaring her and making her jump as she made her way home. Turning the corner by the college and walking straight into a flock of screaming geese had pushed her over the edge. She burst into tears and then sprinted away towards her home.

Sharon wanted to be in the safety and comfort of her bed. She needed a few more hours of sleep at least. Even though she still felt uneasy, she could not run any further. Her body was exhausted, and she felt much older than her years. Sharon breathed heavily as she walked through the underpass, and then she followed the path that would take her to junction road.

As she turned the corner, a masked figure who had been hiding behind a large tree trunk, jumped out in front of her. When Sharon saw what the stranger was holding, she turned to try and run away, but it was already too late. The chainsaw roared to life, and it cut through her right arm like a knife through butter. She screamed in agony as her limb fell to the floor, and then she tripped on a raised tree trunk that was lifting a lump of the tarmac pavement, and she fell face down.

The flat that Brandon had landed in was empty, just as Dufray had told him, but the building felt so odd, that it was giving him the chills. There was a very strange feeling of death here, and it made him shiver. There were no bulbs placed in the light fitments, so it was dark in every room. Brandon felt cold, and he was unsure if this was a result of travelling through the plasma chamber, the eeriness of the building, or if the weather was cold outside. Something felt wrong here, and he wanted to get out of the flat as soon as possible.

He walked over to the window to take a good look outside. The flat was on the ground floor, and from the window, he had a clear view of the underpass across the road. There was a masked figure hidden behind a tree, and they were holding something large up to their chest. Then he noticed the girl as she was about to turn the corner, and she ran straight into the path of the waiting assailant. He could only watch on in horror as the chainsaw sliced easily through the girl's arm.

Part of Brandon wanted to go outside and stop the attack on the girl, but he had minutes left here at most. The attacker was now cutting the girl limb from limb, and she was screaming and making an almost inhuman sound as her legs were cut off at the knee. Brandon had to move fast. He found the way out of the living room and located the front door. It was a simple lock that was easily opened from the inside and thankfully, it did not require a deadlock key.

He snuck out of the door and looked at his watch to time how long it took him to make his way along the gardens to where the attack was taking place. The masked man was far too busy cutting up his victim to notice Brandon vaulting the hedge and crossing the road behind him. He slipped down by the underpass unseen and Brandon checked his watch again. All of these timings were incredibly important if he was going to fix this.

There were two paths from the other end of the underpass, and he had to time how long it would take to walk along both. He completed his calculations and then he made a note of the details on his phone. Now he was ready to return to Dufray's hidden chamber and when he was alone, he would devise a plan to fix this mess once and for all.

Double down.

When Brandon was ready, he pressed the button on his wrist device. The plasma field activated, and Brandon was safely returned to the chamber. Dufray clapped his hands with glee. He could tell by the look on Brandon's face, that he had witnessed the game with his own eyes. The plasma field quickly dissipated from around Brandon's body and then the door to the chamber unlocked and it raised into the starting position.

Brandon looked a little unsteady as he stepped out of the machine, but it was just for show. He didn't want Dufray to know that he felt fine.

"What did you think of the game?" Dufray asked him curiously.

"Your former associates are sick bastards. We need to stop them as soon as possible. I want to be the one who kills Alexander." Brandon demanded.

Dufray was smiling. Brandon was prepared to do his dirty work, and he could watch him squirm and beg for his life.

"I agree. I still want to be there when it happens though. I want to see that son of a bitch Alexander beg and plead for his life before he is removed from the face of the Earth. I have two wrist devices, which will let me come back with you, and I will watch you kill him. I want to see him die." It was clear that Dufray was intent on having his revenge.

Brandon felt happier knowing that Dufray was accepting his proposal, but he still had one question that was playing on his mind.

"How will you know when it is Alexander's turn to go back?"

"You leave that to me. I told you that I have a line of communication within the club. That person can rig the result. I can make sure that when the club next meets, Alexander is the one who is chosen. I hear that she cannot stand him, and she would be happy to see the back of him."

Brandon had to admit that he was impressed at how devious Dufray was. He was a scumbag of the highest order.

"Okay. Tell me a little bit more about the plan. You only have one chamber, so how do you propose to send us both back?"

"That is quite simple. I will send you back first, and you will land in the flat again. I can provide you with a gun to kill Alexander with. I will give you time to get into position. Then I will set the machine to deliver me at the end of the other end of the underpass. I will block his bracelet with a shielding device to stop him from jumping out, and then I will watch as you tell him that you are going to murder him and I can listen while he pleads for his life."

"And when is the next jump going to happen?"

"Two days from now. It is always activated at midday." Dufray was almost licking his lips in anticipation of the end to this saga that had cost him thirty years of his life.

"I'm in. Let's end this game for good." All that Brandon wanted to do, was to stop this poor woman from enduring a brutal death over and over again. He was ready to leave, as he needed to prepare carefully for this one last time jump, and he had to ensure that everything he had planned would work out perfectly, he could not afford any errors, he had to stop this from happening to the girl.

Both barrels

As the light came in through a crack in the curtains, Sharon opened her eyes, stretched her arms above her head, and gave a loud yawn. She had only drunk two glasses of sparkling wine the night before, but her head felt a little fuzzy. It was the first time in a while that she woke up with a smile on her face. She was lying on Debbie's sofa with a duvet on top of her, so she knew that she had fallen asleep during the movie and Debbie had covered her up to keep her comfy.

She looked around the room for a pen and paper and once she found them, she wrote out a little note to say thank you and she drew a smiley face on the end with three kisses underneath. Then she let herself out of the front door. As she walked down the hill toward the town, she was passed by a silver Audi with a personalised registration plate. The last three letters were KOP, so the driver had to be a Liverpool supporter.

Sharon thought that she had seen the car before somewhere, but she could not place it, or the spectacle-wearing driver. Even though it was early, the weather felt slightly warm already, and Sharon felt odd. There was a sense of release growing inside of her and she felt truly happy and ready to face the day. It felt good to be alive.

Payback

On the following Wednesday, everything was set. Both Brandon and Dufray were waiting at the facility when the text message arrived. Alexander had been confirmed as the player who had won the draw. He would be jumping back to try and achieve the perfect score in the next few minutes. Dufray had already set the machine to transport Brandon back in readiness, and both men now had the return devices strapped onto their wrists.

“I am sending you into the empty flat five minutes before he arrives. Alexander won’t see you as he will land on the path in front of you. It will give you the element of surprise, and you can get to him before he gets to the girl. I will arrive at the duck pond at the same time as Alexander meets the girl. I will see everything in front of me.”

“Let’s make sure that we end this right now,” Brandon said, and Dufray passed him a gun.

“I want him to suffer just like I suffered.” Dufray had a wide grin on his face as he relished the chance to see his nemesis die.

“Oh, he will. Trust me. He will.” Brandon said, and then he climbed into the machine. As Dufray walked over to the controls, Brandon used the small window of opportunity available and he dropped the gun to the side of the chamber so that it was hidden out of sight. Dufray wasn't looking at him and had not seen a thing. Brandon still didn't trust Dufray. He was prepared for all eventualities though.

The machine activated and the lid closed, and Brandon closed his eyes and felt the plasma surge around him before he was sent back to the flat. He had very little time from the moment he arrived, but he needed to find the right position to deal with the problem. A few minutes later, Dufray stepped into the machine for the first time in many years.

He was driven by revenge, and this time he was determined to make Alexander pay for his betrayal. When he returned, he was jumping back into the clubhouse where he would claim his prize and destroy their machine. He was never going to let anyone destroy his machine. That was an issue he was happy to deal with himself. He placed a fully loaded gun in his pocket, and he waited patiently as the machine engaged automatically, and then his jump began.

After landing in the empty flat, Brandon made his way straight toward the front door. Every second counted now. He checked his weapon before he opened the door, and everything was as it should be. As he stepped outside, the sun was shining. He had studied maps from the area published around the time, and there was only one place that he could be waiting to enact his plan. He sprinted across the road to get himself in place and ready to hide away from the target.

Sharon turned the corner by the college and a group of Canadian geese squawked noisily at her, making her jump. She laughed at how stupid she felt being scared by the birds. She walked through the middle of them, and they quickly spread apart clearing her a pathway. She was almost home and looking forward to heading back to sleep in the comfort of her bed. As she turned the corner, she made her way over the wooden bridge that spanned the river.

The morning sun was glinting on the ripples of the water as the river was flowing underneath it. Sharon stood still for a few seconds while leaning on the guard side rail in the middle of the bridge. She never had the chance to stop and enjoy nature normally, and just breathing in the morning air made it feel good to be alive. After taking a few minutes to herself, she began a slow walk towards the underpass.

As Sharon moved forward, she was still wearing a beaming smile on her face. As she cleared the other side of the bridge, she could see a man who was running down the path. He looked like he was heading straight for her, and he was carrying something in his hand. It looked like a samurai blade, and now he raised it aloft as he charged down the path in her direction.

Alexander was determined to slice the girl up into small pieces, and he was sure that this would achieve a perfect score. Sharon was just about to turn around and run when she heard a gunshot ringing out through the air. Then Sharon heard an inhuman-sounding wailing. Brandon had shot through Alexander's raised hand, destroying his palm in the process.

Alexander panicked as he saw Brandon moving towards him with a raised gun in his hand. He tried to use the return jump device and he pushed the emergency button frantically to try and use it to escape, but it was futile. He did not know that the device was being jammed by Dufray, and there was no way back to safety for him. He would have to suffer before a rescue mission could be sent back to rescue him.

Alexander walked toward Brandon. He was desperate to try and plead for his life.

"Whatever it is that you want, I can give it to you. Money, power, fame? Whatever it is, I can make it happen! Just, please don't kill me. Please spare my life. I have a family!" He begged.

Sharon was desperate to get away from these maniacs, but as she turned around, yet another man was approaching her from the other side of the underpass. He too was holding a gun in his hand. There was no way out for her. She was trapped between the armed stranger in a dark coat who looked extremely odd, the man who had been carrying a sword, and now a third man was holding a gun and pointing it her way.

She had been convinced that today was going to be a good day, and now she was unsure how much time she had left to live. Sharon froze on the spot, and she closed her eyes, if she was going to die, she prayed that it would be swift and as painless as possible. She started to pray in silence for a saviour, unaware that a saviour was already in her midst.

The gun that Brandon held, was pointed straight at Alexander's head, but he continued to edge his way closer towards Brandon. Alexander could see that the stranger had a time jump return device fitted to his wrist and knowing that he was a time traveller too offered him some hope. His return device had malfunctioned, and now he needed to obtain the device from the gunman's wrist and get the hell out of here, but he had to convince the man to deal with him first.

"Tell me, what can I offer you that would make your dreams come true?" Alexander asked Brandon, who was watching him moving closer by the second.

"That's far enough. Step back and move into the underpass. I have someone with me who wants to have a little chat with you." Brandon told him. He wasn't open to any negotiations. Alexander raised his one good hand in the air sheepishly and did as he was told.

Dufray was waiting in the underpass and as Alexander turned the corner, it took him a few seconds to recognise the ageing man that stood on the path before him.

"You! I know you. But you are dead? I know you are dead because I killed you myself!" He was confused about how this could happen. Dufray's face was growing redder by the second as his anger levels rose.

"No, you didn't kill me. You just left me for dead. Now I've come back to see you pay for what you did to me. Thirty long years I have waited for this moment. Now that I have heard you squirm, and plead for mercy, that is good enough for me. I want you to shoot him now, Brandon." Dufray ordered.

A gunshot rang out through the underpass, and Sharon had to open her eyes. She was scared, but she had to see what was happening and know who had just been shot.

She felt no pain in her body and that was a good sign that she wasn't the target.

Dufray dropped to his knees with blood flowing from a wound to the right-hand side of his skull. He looked in shock at the betrayal despite his own intention to betray Brandon and leave him here. He fell forward and was unable to move his limbs as temporary paralysis set in. Brandon moved over to where he lay, and he removed the return device from Dufray's wrist.

Alexander was smiling.

"Good man. Now give it to me! I promise you more money than you have ever dreamed possible!" Alexander pleaded. Instead of giving the device to Alexander, he passed the device over to Sharon instead.

"If you want to live, put this on your wrist. You have to trust me." He told her.

The man had saved her life, but she was totally confused. She took the device and did as she was told. She placed it around her wrist and tightened it securely. Alexander was shaking his head in disbelief at what he had witnessed.

"You bloody fool. I could have given you anything that you wanted!" He was shaking his head in disbelief. He wasn't used to not getting his own way.

"Oh, you will give me what I want. You see I do have a dream, and that dream is a world free of parasites like you. Do you think that just because you have money, you can get away with murder? My dream is to rid the world of scumbags like you." Brandon told him, and then he raised the gun so that it was level with Alexander's face.

Sensing that he had run out of options, Alexander went to stand up in a last-ditch effort to charge at Brandon. He had been waiting for the perfect moment and Brandon fired the gun shooting Alexander straight through the middle of the forehead. As he fell back onto the pavement, Alexander's brains sprayed out from the back of his skull.

"Come back from that one," Brandon told him.

Sharon remained frozen to the spot with her back to the wall of the underpass. She had just seen two men shot down in cold blood right in front of her, and there were blood splatters all over her clothes. Now she was the last one left and she feared for her life.

"Please don't kill me!" She begged as she turned to face Brandon.

"It's ok. You are safe now. I know this must be confusing and this is going to sound more than a little bit crazy, but let me explain what was about to happen to you."

Brandon walked over to Dufray who was bleeding from the wound to the side of his head.

"This piece of shit here is called Dufray. He joined that blonde scumbag over there in a club for eccentric rich arseholes who found a way to travel back in time. You were their sole target. They knew that you were supposed to die today, so they could keep coming back over and over again to murder you in a twisted game.

The sole object of their game was to murder you in horrific ways until one of them achieved a perfect score. The members all took it, in turn, to come back and slaughter you. It was just a challenge to them."

Brandon kicked Dufray as hard as he could as the man lay on the floor, and he moaned loudly as he felt a rib crack. He then went through Dufray's pockets until he found the signal blocker, and he deactivated it and placed it safely in his pocket. "This rich arsehole paid me to come back and murder his killer. Then he was going to kill me. Neither of them cared about your pain or suffering. It was all just a game to him too."

"What the fuck are you talking about?" Sharon had heard his story, but it was too fantastical to be true. She still had no idea what was going on here at all.

The man in front of her was still holding a gun in his hand. Sharon was afraid that she would be his next victim, but his story made no sense. He held his hands up to try and assure her that he meant her no harm.

“I didn't come here to kill you, Sharon. I came here to save you, and I can prove it to you.”

“How on Earth are you going to that, and how the hell do you know my name?” She asked. There was no way that she was going to run, so she would try and humour the man until help arrived, or she had a chance to make her escape.

He knew that Sharon would be overwhelmed, but he was running out of time. Brandon had to show her that he was telling her the truth.

"We all came back here from thirty years in the future." He went over and kicked the corpse of Alexander so hard in the ribs that some trapped air escaped from his lungs, "Attached to this arseholes arm, there is a device that enables him to return home. In a few minutes, I'm going to press it to activate the homing beacon and send him back to the clubhouse.

Before I activate the beacon, I need you to turn around and watch. In just over a minute, a drunk driver will speed along the road in a silver Jaguar. You are meant to be hit by the car, and it would kill you outright, except I'm going to go against all the rules of time travel and I will change the timeline to give you a different future, but only if you will let me. Otherwise, they will come back and correct this timeline, save Alexander, and you will continue to die over and over again at their hands."

In some strange way, this fantastical story seemed to make sense. The man knew her name. He had plenty of opportunities to kill Sharon if he wanted to, but he hadn't shot her, and he looked out of place in this decade. His clothes were all wrong, and the technology on the dead man's wrist looked to be far ahead of its time. If this was real, and making this decision was the one thing that meant she could live, then she was going to take her chance.

“Ok. Show me,” Sharon said, and then she turned around.

Brandon lifted the injured Dufray from the ground, and he groaned as Brandon placed him over his shoulder. He carried the injured man over the path and then dumped him in the middle of the road. Brandon stood back as Dufray tried to climb up onto his knees, but he was too weak to stand.

Right on time, and just as Brandon had predicted, the silver-coloured Jaguar flew past on the road in front of them both. The speed limit on this stretch of road was set at thirty miles per hour, and this car must have been going over seventy miles an hour at least. The car skidded as it came to the bend, and it almost tipped over as it flew around the blind bend.

The car struck Dufray just as he managed to lift himself upright, and it sent him flying over the bonnet. It took the driver seconds to regain control of the vehicle, and Sharon shivered as she felt a chill running down her spine. She would have been walking across that road at around the exact time, and the driver would not have seen her.

“Fuck. You were telling me the truth. He would have mowed me down!” She said out loud. Then they both watched as the driver carried on as if nothing had happened and he fled the scene as quickly as he could.

“I know. I've seen you die in a far worse way. They once cut you into pieces with a chainsaw.” Brandon told her.

Sharon was in a state of shock. She had no idea that a few quiet drinks with her friend would lead to something as life-changing as this. She was becoming angry, and it was unrelenting as the hatred towards the club members continued to build inside of her.

“Now, we have a little bit of a problem,” Brandon said, and Sharon knew that she wasn't going to like what he was about to tell her.

“I don't like the sound of that, but I guess you better tell me what it is.”

“The problem I have now is that you should be dead. You would no longer exist in this timeline. Whatever you do from this point on will affect the future, and if we don’t do something, then the results could be catastrophic. So, as I see it, you have just two choices open to you.”

“Go on...” Sharon wasn’t sure that she wanted to hear any more, but she had no choice in the matter.

“The first option is that I can shoot you now and we can leave this timeline unaffected, which I’d prefer not to do. Or, there is a second alternative. You don't have a lot of time to decide though.”

"Then I guess you better tell me what the second option is then." Sharon was positive that whatever it was, she would prefer this option over the first.

A brief history of time.

Brandon knelt next to Alexander's body. Sharon watched carefully as he activated the return on the device and then he held the button down. He just managed to jump out of the way as the plasma field surrounded Alexander's body, and a few seconds later, the body had been sent forward in time.

"Wow. Is it that simple?" Sharon asked.

"It might make you feel a bit sick for a while, but not straight away. It's your call though. You can stay if you want?"

"I think the future sounds a little more interesting," Sharon replied. After discovering that she had died so many times before, she was now determined to live.

Wherever you will go.

After watching Alexander's body being transported into the future, Sharon was ready to take her turn. She pressed and held the button on her wrist and the return device was activated. the future was about to be re-written. The jump had been activated and as a new future was not yet written for her, she saw time strings that were spiralling all around her body as the plasma covered her skin.

Sharon watched in awe as her body was engulfed in plasma and a brilliant blue pulse surrounded her. She could see shadows of humanity moving all around her. She could only compare the journey as akin to walking along a never-ending railway platform and the faces of the people aged as they walked toward her. Some of them withered away to dust, while others walked off in different directions.

The journey through time was both beautiful and frightening in equal measure. She would arrive at her destination soon, and she knew exactly what she was going to do when she made it into the clubhouse.

The members of the perfect kill club drank champagne and ate caviar and oysters as they waited with bated breath for the latest news update. Olivia checked her watch and saw that it was almost time for the scoring to take place.

“Can I ask you to take your seats, please? Let's hope for a really good score this time!” She shouted. The members started strolling back to their chairs with glasses in hand. “I now have confirmation that the newsreel has changed, so please have your tablets ready for you to score the kill.”

Olivia pressed the play button, and the familiar reporter began to speak on the screen.

“Police are still trying to locate the whereabouts of nineteen-year-old Sharon Tasker. The young woman had last been seen in the early hours of Sunday morning this week, close to a hit and run that left an unknown male with life-changing injuries. The woman was last seen by a paper boy before seemingly disappearing into thin air. Police are asking for anyone else who may have seen her walking in the area, to come forward.”

Sensing that something had gone badly wrong and that they may have to go back and correct another mistake, Olivia looked pale as she paused the news segment.

"Oh no. It appears that something has gone wrong. We need to send another clean-up team in. Marcus, I need you to get prepped for an emergency jump. We must do everything that we can to go back and save poor Alexander." Marcus was one of the most experienced members of the club. He jumped up from his chair excitedly, as he was more than ready to go back and fix the errors in the timeline.

The members were all talking noisily amongst themselves as they made their way towards the room containing the transportation tunnel. When they stepped inside, the warning light became active advising that a return was already in progress and the cylinder door remained closed. The blue lights flashed inside the chamber to announce an imminent arrival.

"Alexander's coming back!" Marcus shouted. There was a nervous wait, and after a few minutes, the door of the machine opened and the hazy cloud inside began to clear.

"Alexander!" Olivia shouted, and then Alexander's lifeless body fell forward onto the floor sending sprays of blood over all the members present. "No!" Olivia screamed.

Two of the male members of the club dashed forward and lifted Alexander from the floor.

“Get him up onto a table in the other room. We need to get a doctor here urgently.” Olivia screamed. Between them, the men carried Alexander into the scoring room while the other members cleaned away the plates of food and glasses and then helped to lift him onto the table.

One of the women placed two of her fingers on the side of Alexander’s neck.

“There’s no pulse. So, whatever you are going to do, you better hurry!” She pleaded. Olivia was already on the phone and calling the group’s Doctor, but the ringing tone continued, and the Doctor wasn’t answering his phone. She was beginning to regret fixing the result for her secret donor, and she felt guilty that Alexander had been hurt. If anyone found out, then she would face expulsion, or even worse.

“I’m trying to! Marcus are you ready to go back yet? We must try and fix this quickly!” She shouted.

“Almost! I am just going to grab a weapon. Then you can send me back.” He replied as he placed a return device around his wrist.

Marcus started moving quickly towards the launching room, ready to wait for Olivia to activate the machine and to send him back to correct the mistakes before they could happen.

Boo!

As Marcus stepped into the room, he noticed something odd. The door of the tunnel was still open. It would normally close after the traveller had exited the chamber to move into a self-decontamination mode, and it could only be opened by use of the control panel, or from the exit button inside of the tunnel. He had seen the door closing with his own eyes, and something felt wrong. He was just about to turn around and alert the others when he felt a stinging sensation on the top of his head.

Something was running down the back of Marcus's neck, and he instinctively placed his hands on the top of his head. There was a large object protruding from the top of his skull, and he had to use both of his hands to pull it out. It was a long-bladed, serrated hunting knife that was covered in blood. He stumbled forwards as the blood gushed from the wound to his head, and he felt very dizzy and sure that he was about to pass out.

His eyesight was becoming hazy, and Marcus struggled to focus on the figure in front of him. At the very last moment, he recognized the face of the person who was standing in front of him, but it couldn't be her.

"You!" He said, just before he fell to the floor. He would be dead within minutes.

The door to the viewing room opened, but no one was paying any attention to what was going on behind them. Olivia had assured the members of the club that as soon as they could get hold of the doctor, he would be on his way to help. If the Doctor couldn't fix this, then Marcus would have to go back further and clean up properly. The beauty of time travel was that it enabled them to fix any errors, but sometimes it needed some careful calculations. They would just go back slightly earlier and make everything good again.

Mrs Beckworth looked worried as she faced Olivia. She was just about to protest at how badly this error was being handled, afraid that Alexander might suffer unnecessarily.

"My dear girl.." She began and then a gunshot rang out around the room. Pieces of brain flew out of the hole in the front of her head and the fragments of brain, blood and bone showered Olivia's face. She froze in fear as Mrs Beckworth went to touch the back of her head, only to realise that half of her brain was now missing. "Oh my." These were her final words before she too fell dead to the floor.

The silence in the room was soon replaced with screaming and pandemonium ensued as more shots were fired at random toward the other guests who were present. All of the members started shouting and screaming as they ran towards the exit door. It made life so much easier for Sharon as she lifted the other weapon that she had chosen from the cupboard, and she began firing the pump-action shotgun toward the gathered crowd. Considering how sick and twisted this execution was, she was surprised at how much she was enjoying taking out her revenge on these warped bastards.

The bodies soon piled up in front of the door, blocking the remaining members from exiting the club. Sharon would not stop until every single member of this depraved group had been gunned down. This was more than just revenge for all the times that they had murdered her; it was payback for every time that these bastards had exploited people whom they considered beneath them, and they held with utter contempt.

The world would be a much better place without them. The last shot rang out, and then there was silence as the last of the members fell to the floor gasping for breath. Finally, there was nothing but silence as the metallic smell of discharged ammunition filled the room. Sharon stood and surveyed the carnage in front of her, and for some strange reason, the scene looked like a giant twisted work of art that belonged on display in a gallery.

The buzzer rang, and it shook Sharon from her daze. It took her some time to find the button that opened the gate, but she soon located it and allowed the car to enter the driveway. She let Brandon inside. He had fuel cans in the car, and they were placed all around the mansion to destroy the evidence.

When the pair were satisfied that the place would become an inferno, they walked out of the front door together. Brandon lit a box of matches and threw it over his shoulder into the hallway behind him. The flames began to take hold as the car made its way back along the drive, and Sharon leaned back over her car seat. The flames were growing wildly as the petrol canisters exploded, and the time travel chamber began to crack and melt from the intense heat.

“So, now that those bastards are all dead, what shall we do next?” Sharon asked. Brandon turned his head and smiled at her.

“I’ve been thinking about that. I think we deserve a little fun. How about, we get you cleaned up? Then go for a bite to eat. I have a crazy idea that I want to run by you, and I think that you might like it.” Sharon began to feel the excitement building inside of her. This was her first day of experiencing the future, and so far, she was loving it.

Eat the rich

The main door of the hospital was open. It was visiting time between three and five in the afternoon and Brandon walked straight in without anyone challenging him. It wasn't difficult to find the man that he was looking for, and he was positive that it would all be worth it this time. He made his way along the corridors toward the end-of-life care section.

The machines were bleeping continuously as he walked into the private room and over to the side of the bed. The elderly patient unexpectedly opened his eyes, and he recognised the visitor in his room. His mouth was dry as he spoke.

"Thirty long years I've waited for you, and finally you arrive. Have you come here to taunt me, you double-crossing bastard?"

"Thirty years? It felt like hours to me," Brandon smirked.

"You son of a bitch. You left me back there lying on the road in agony. My back was broken, and I have been paralysed in both legs since, thanks to your betrayal."

"You got what karma had in store for you. I hope you suffered as much as you all made that poor girl suffer."

Brandon would have loved to shut this guy up permanently, but he had to remain calm.

“She was going to die anyway you fucking idiot!” The elderly patient shouted and then started to cough. Splatters of blood sprayed from his mouth and into his hand.

On the monitor above the bed, the rate of the patient’s heartbeat increased by around twenty beats a minute.

“Put me out of my misery or get out of here before I call in the nurse and have you removed,” Dufray demanded.

“I’m glad that you have suffered for all of this time,” Brandon replied.

“I could have made you rich you fool!”

“Some things are worth more than money. I will enjoy watching you die again.”

Dufray had heard enough. He pressed the alarm buzzer repeatedly to summon the nurse. The light in the hallway outside flashed and the nurse turned the light off before she walked along the hallway and entered the room. Once she was inside, she locked the door behind her.

“Thank God you are here nurse. You need to remove this man. He is an unwanted trespasser. I want you to call the police and have him arrested.” Dufray demanded. The nurse looked up at the heart rate monitor, and she took the emergency call button out of the hand of the patient and placed it safely out of his reach.

"Please Mr Dufray, you need to calm down. This stress is not good for your body. The last thing we need is for you to die of another heart attack again." The nurse told him.

The nurse then turned around to speak to Brandon.

"Are you staying to watch again?" She asked him.

"I wouldn't miss it for the world." He smiled.

Dufray tried to edge his way up in the bed, but Brandon pushed him down by the shoulders and placed his hand over the old man's mouth. The nurse then walked over to the side of the room and opened a cupboard. She removed an object from inside of it and plugged it in at the wall.

"What is today's big surprise going to be then?" Brandon asked her. The nurse switched on the item, and she pulled down her face mask and smiled as she pulled the trigger on the item that she was holding, and it whirred noisily into life.

"Today, we will be operating on the patient using the bone saw. The patient has a tumour on his brain, and we need to go in quickly. There is no time for us to administer any anaesthetic I'm afraid."

The nurse moved over to the side of the bed, and it was only now that Dufray finally recognised the face of the nurse, and his eyes became wide with fright.

"The patient has to give us his consent," Brandon told her, and he shook Dufray's head forward and backwards in his hands. "Permission granted."

"I'm afraid that this might sting a little bit," Sharon said as she moved the bone saw down, and his skull began to splinter as she began to cut into Dufray's forehead. The elderly man screamed into Brandon's hands, as pieces of his skull were cut away in segments. He suffered a great deal at Sharon's hands before his heart gave out and he finally passed away.

"I did the best that I could, but I'm afraid that the operation was not successful on this occasion," Sharon said.

"Never mind. We can go back and try again tomorrow." Brandon replied with a smirk.

When Sharon and Brandon had changed into clean clothes, Sharon unlocked the door and peered out into the corridor. It was clear. It was always clear at this time of day. Sharon walked out, closely followed by Brandon. They were leaving a scene of total carnage behind them. Blood was dripping from every wall, and Sharon locked the door behind them both.

It would be another two hours before anyone entered the room and discovered the remains of the patient, by that time they would be far away from the hospital. The couple both walked slowly out towards the exit of the hospital together.

"That was a very inventive kill today," Brandon said, praising Sharon on her choice of weapon.

"Thank you. Shall we pay him another visit at the same time tomorrow?"

"Definitely. But I think you mean yesterday."

Sharon chuckled.

"You know what I mean."

"How many more times do you want to murder him?" Brandon asked.

"Let's keep going until we find the perfect way to kill him," Sharon replied.

"I have a better idea." Brandon had a mischievous look on his face.

"Well, don't keep me in suspense, let's hear it then!" She looked excited.

"What about we go back into the past and kill every member of the club? Stop them before they have a chance to breed. End the family timeline so that their offspring can never follow suit."

Sharon looked deep in thought, but then it all seemed to make sense to her.

“I think that is a great idea, but by doing that, you will be going against your ethics and changing the future.”

“I know. Karma really can be a bitch sometimes though. See you at the club tomorrow?” He asked her. She nodded excitedly and smiled, and then they both walked off in separate directions. Tomorrow they would start to change the timelines for all the families of the club’s former members.

Epilogue.

No more heroes anymore.

The time overseer had witnessed enough senseless torture. He set his time portal device for the correct space and time in history, and he activated the return. Part of what was once a man called Nikola Tesla landed in the underground hideaway where Dufray's machine was being used daily. The couple who were using it had a good reason for wanting revenge, but Tesla could not allow their game to continue any longer.

Dufray was dead, and now he would remain dead where he could rot in hell. From far in the future, Tesla had watched as little ripples in time emerged and now, he had come back to destroy the machine that he had created. It was far too dangerous to allow anyone to use it anymore.

This was not the Nikola Tesla of old. This was a Tesla from the year 2150. His body had been frozen long ago, and when the technology of the future had developed far enough, he was given a new lease of life thanks to the organic nanobots that had repaired every dead cell in his body. In time, he had chosen to have his consciousness uploaded to the second version of the metaverse, but now and again he would make his way back in time by using an artificial body to correct humanity's errors.

Tesla had been sickened by the way humanity had descended into a chaotic breed and he had taken the decision to have his consciousness uploaded to a new electronic universe over a hundred years after the Third World War had ended. Humanity had come to live as one which was a necessity for their very survival, and everyone worked as part of a collective mind.

Tesla planted a small teleportation device on the time travel machine, and then he activated it. The machine was sent to his lab, far in the future where he could safely destroy it. When Brandon and Sharon next visited so they could use the machine, they would arrive at a mystery that would never be solved. Tesla paused and took in the air into his artificial lungs before he activated his return. It was much dirtier air back here, and he was disappointed to see that mankind still had no respect for the only planet they had.

Tesla had recently uploaded the consciousness of a pigeon. The conversation between them had been disappointing so far as the bird was constantly thinking, of food and sex, but Tesla wasn't giving up on the bird yet. He pushed the button on his device, and his brief visit to the past was now over. He was going back to where he belonged, to a world of never-ending knowledge and peace, and very brief and unrewarding conversations with pigeons.

www.ingramcontent.com/pod-product-compliance
Lightning Source LLC
LaVergne TN
LVHW010107170826
845678LV00012B/2289

9798848845129